What the critics are saying:

"Katherine Kingston paints an accurate, vivid picture of life in medieval England. I not only enjoyed the great setting, but the emotionally charged characters as well. This is a perfect sit-by-the-pool summer read!"- *Nadine St. Denis for Romance Junkies*

"As a fan of medieval romance, I fully enjoyed reading Healing Passion… The author painted a striking portrait of Lady Juliana and Sir Thomas. The secrecy at the Keep was a living, breathing entity, a character in its own right…."- *Rho, A Romance Review*

"Healing Passion exemplifies Ms. Kingston's skill as an erotic historical writer. This story is fantastic with its rich melding of erotic and historical elements confirming that two people can rise above what fate has dealt them and revel in true love… This wonderful medieval story is a true gem and a definite keeper."-*Aggie Tsirikas, Just Erotic Romance Reviews*

HEALING PASSION

Katherine Kingston

HEALING PASSION
An Ellora's Cave Publication, December 2004

Ellora's Cave Publishing, Inc.
PO Box 787
Hudson, OH 44236-0787

ISBN #1-4199-5119-X

ISBN MS Reader (LIT) ISBN # 1-84360-956-8
Other available formats (no ISBNs are assigned):
Adobe (PDF), Rocketbook (RB), Mobipocket (PRC) & HTML

Edited by *Briana St. James*
Cover art by *Syneca*

HEALING PASSION

Katherine Kingston

Chapter One

"Sir Thomas? Are you sure a messenger was sent to Groswick to inform them of our coming?"

Thomas shook himself out of an exhausted half-doze and followed his squire Ralf's line of sight straight ahead to where their destination loomed. The reason for the question was clear.

The place looked incredibly forbidding, inhospitable, and unwelcoming.

The huge, dark, stone fortress had a four-story main keep surrounded by a two-story wall. The remote setting, with the keep hedged in on two sides by hills and accessed by a road through a narrow pass to the gate, contributed to the feeling. Even as they approached, an enormous portcullis remained adamantly closed over a heavy wood door. No movement or greeting of any kind indicated they'd been spotted or would be welcomed.

Thomas was used to being greeted with courtesy, and sometimes even with elaborate pomp and ceremony. He didn't favor excessive display, but the complete lack of welcome here dismayed him. This mission had already taken too much time and too much travel.

"The herald said his message had been delivered." Thomas sighed and rubbed at his throbbing head. He just wanted to be done with this Groswick affair. He was close to thirty, getting too old for this, though his friends would laugh did they ever hear him say so. His tired bones wanted rest. But even more, his spirit craved a place to call home. Not so much a place, though, he realized, probing feelings kept long buried as one would test a damaged tooth to see how much pain it could cause. He wanted family, people he could settle with and become close to. He longed for peace, order, a secure and comfortable place to lay his head at night.

Once before, he'd had all that, but a woman's lies had torn apart and destroyed it. Now, however, after two years spent watching his closest friends find comfort and happiness in marriage to extraordinary ladies, the seed that had lain dormant for so long sprouted and began to unfurl. He wanted what they had, or at least some reasonable shadow of it.

Both of his closest friends had found unusual and special women to fill their hearts. Women who could love and submit freely to their husbands, yet still be strong, brave, and intelligent. They'd had to be. Lady Rosalind and Lady Mary had each survived terrible things and come through desperate tests, emerging stronger and wiser from them.

He sighed and set those thoughts aside. For now he faced the problem of entrance into this dreary and shuttered keep. He expected at any moment to see the portcullis rise in acknowledgement of his arrival. No one could think one knight traveling with only his squire and one other vassal represented any threat. But though they rode up close to the gate and stopped there, nothing happened.

The drizzle turned into a full-bore rain as the gray remains of the day faded into twilight. Thomas watched the wall around the gate and the guard tower over it. He caught periodic flashes of movement. The place wasn't deserted, and their presence must have been noted.

After waiting a good while, Thomas rode forward, signaling his companions to remain behind. He stopped just below the gate.

"Greetings! I am Sir Thomas of Carlwick. I come in peace, in the name of the king." He shouted, trying to make the words as forceful as they were loud. "Open for the king's representative."

He backed away, rejoining Ralf and Bertram. Again they waited, expecting that the order would bring quick action. It didn't.

His helmet kept most of the rain off his face, but the moisture still leaked beneath his chain mail byrnie and soaked his undergarments. Daylight was fading quickly, and he had no wish to spend the night camped out on the plain.

When his patience wore out, he rode forward again. "I am Sir Thomas of Carlwick. I represent the king. Admit me or risk the king's wrath and the weight of his might on you."

On the rampart above the gate and in the guardhouse, figures scurried around. After another pause long enough to set him grinding his teeth, a metallic screech finally signaled their impending admission. Nonetheless, they still had to linger another fifteen minutes in the drenching rain while the portcullis creaked upward and the heavy wood gates swung ponderously open.

He was in no good humor when they were finally able to enter the grounds. They stopped in the bailey. A groom and a pair of stable boys came forward and assisted them to dismount, then took charge of their horses.

A man in livery appeared at the top of the stairs that clung to the side of the keep wall, standing at the main door, waiting to invite them in. Weary to the bone, they climbed the steps and stood before the servant.

"I'm Sir Thomas of Carlwick," he announced again. "My squire, Ralf and my man, Bertram." The servant bowed.

"Enter and be at peace, Sir Thomas," the man invited. "I'll announce your arrival to Lady Juliana."

Instead of letting directly into the main hall, the door gave into an anteroom, where Sir Thomas removed his helm and shook rain off his cloak. Perhaps it was the gloomy weather outside or the fact that only two torches in high brackets illuminated the area, but the tall, undecorated stone walls of the entranceway loomed forbiddingly and the whole had an air of mourning or despair.

The man led them into the great hall, announcing Sir Thomas's arrival as they entered. Here the atmosphere lightened. More torches brightened the area, assisted by the blazing fire, which burned in an enormous fireplace on a side wall. The aromas of roasted meat, fresh-baked bread, and ale assaulted him and set his stomach rumbling. For all that, though, no more than two dozen people occupied a room which could easily have held a hundred or more. The table on the dais at the far end was empty.

A woman rose from the center of the side table where most of the people gathered and approached him. Her clothes were of good quality cloth, though plain, and she wore a simple cap on her head. She was young, very pretty, and carried herself with regal grace.

"Sir Thomas," she said, dropping into a deep curtsy. "Welcome to Castle Groswick. I'm Lady Juliana. I regret we kept you waiting so long in the rain, but I fear we were unprepared for visitors, and the guards on duty have little experience. They knew not what to do and perforce needed to confer with their superiors prior to making a decision to admit you." Her voice was sweet, but had a surprisingly rough, hoarse undertone.

She looked at him closely, no doubt noticing how the rain plastered his hair to his head and dripped off his nose and armor. "Please come close to the fire and dry off, Sir Thomas. Your men, also. Quarters are being prepared for you even now, but as we were not told the date of your coming, it will be some time yet before they're ready."

She moved toward the large fireplace, and he followed, with Ralf and Bertram behind him. The warmth washed over and soothed him as they approached the blaze. It mitigated some of his anger. Thomas stripped off his gauntlets and rubbed his cold hands together near the fire.

"I've sent for mulled wine and food for you as well," the lady said. "As you see we're a small household, but we do try to receive guests hospitably."

A servant appeared bearing a tray with cups and a pitcher of steaming liquid. The aroma—the tang of wine laced with cinnamon and other fragrant spices—hit him forcibly in the gut.

Lady Juliana poured out the mixture into a cup, which she brought to him.

Their hands met as he took the cup from her. Warmth flowed from the clay vessel into the palms he wrapped around it, a blessed, welcome heat. Something else flowed into his fingers in the places where they touched Lady Juliana's, a warmth of a different kind. It sparked and tingled, sending a river of fire through his veins and into his loins. His cock took notice and stood immediately to attention.

Thomas smothered a groan as he fought the reaction. He'd gone years with no more than the occasional meaningless joining. Only once since Margaret's betrayal had he felt the stirrings of anything beyond physical need, and the woman who'd provoked it was married to his closest friend. Was he doomed to be roused only by those beyond his reach? This lady was married as well, and any attraction to her could only complicate his mission and his life. But she was a lovely woman, with a slender, graceful figure, and glossy, dark brown curls escaping from her cap to give her a winsome air.

He drew a deep breath and looked down into the cup before he sipped, watching the way the darkish liquid swirled as he tipped it. He took a drink and didn't have to feign enjoyment or relief. The flavor matched the aroma, a sharp brew of fermented fruit laced with the taste-pleasing enhancements of the spices. It warmed his mouth and spread the heat all the way down as he drank deeper. Tense muscles, especially in his shoulders and back, began to loosen and relax.

He closed his eyes for a moment to relish the taste of the liquid and the feel of the warmth. When he opened them again, he made the mistake of meeting Lady Juliana's gaze directly.

Her eyes were an unusual light blue/green shade, large, clear, and direct. They sparkled with her smile of welcome for him, but... Surely it was his imagination that led him to think he saw another world of emotion just below the surface. Yet he would swear he found in her gaze an innate strength, endurance, courage, shades of sorrow or grief, and more... Oh, no, he didn't need or want to see that. He could admire the passion she held in firm check, but he would have to take care to avoid it. She belonged to another man—if that man were still alive, something he had begun to doubt.

He pulled his gaze away from her eyes and let it roam the rest of her face. Her fine, clear, pale skin bore a few light freckles, mostly around her slim nose. They didn't damage her looks at all. The scars did, unfortunately, though the beautiful line of cheek and jaw drew attention away from them and almost nullified their effect.

The uglier of the two was a line that curved from just above her left cheekbone to her temple. Even though it showed tiny circular marks on either side of the scar where it had been stitched closed, it was still almost a quarter-inch-width of whitish flesh. The other was a narrower, straighter line from almost the middle of her chin up and across to an inch or so beyond the corner of her mouth. The pinker coloration suggested it was a more recent addition.

Oddly, he found they increased rather than destroyed her attractiveness. The newer one bracketed her lips and emphasized their lovely curve and rich pink color. They marked her as a woman who'd experienced some of life's darker side rather than a naïve young girl.

He didn't think he'd shown any reaction to the scars, but after a moment her lips tightened and some of the sparkle faded from her eyes, so apparently she'd noticed something. The scars looked like many he'd seen on men following a battle, which made him wonder how they came to be on the face of a young and otherwise lovely woman. Something about her bearing said she would not want to talk of them.

He took another long drink of the mulled wine. Moments later more servants approached bearing platters of food.

"Sir Thomas, if you and your men will have a seat, the food is here."

Platters of meat sliced from a roast fowl, salted pork, and freshly baked bread were placed before them along with bowls of roasted tubers and boiled greens. The aromas emanating from them had his stomach rumbling and mouth watering long before the first bite hit his tongue.

"Pass on my compliments to your cook," Thomas said around a piece of meat so savory he couldn't remember when he'd last eaten anything so good. The lady ran her household well if the quality of food and service were any indication.

Lady Juliana nodded and went to talk to a servant for a moment. When she returned, she sat down on the opposite side of the table from him.

"I trust you're feeling somewhat better now, Sir Thomas," she said.

He looked up and nodded. She drew a deep breath as though getting ready to speak, but she let it out again on a long sigh. He watched her pick up a cup of wine and put it down when her hands shook so hard she couldn't keep the liquid from sloshing over. Was it just his presence that made her so nervous? Unexpected guests? Or did she feel the same sense of connection he'd noticed when they'd touched?

An older woman toddled into the room and straight to his side. She was short and hunched over, with a wrinkled face and rheumy eyes whose color might once have been the same as Lady Juliana's.

"I heard we had guests just arrived," the old woman said, staring hard at Thomas. She was very close and her eyes narrowed in a squint, so she probably couldn't see very well anymore. Her breath came in harsh, wheezing pants. "Who be you, sirrah?"

"Mother!" Lady Juliana drew a sharp breath. "This is Sir Thomas of Carlwick, come here from the king. Sir Thomas, may I present my mother, Lady Ardsley."

Thomas stood to bow to the lady, and found himself towering so high over her, he was looking down on the top of her head until she craned her neck to stare up at him. "Lady Ardsley," he acknowledged.

"Sir Thomas, is it?" she asked. The old lady nudged the occupant of a nearby chair and the young man obliged by sliding down to the next seat, giving his place up to her. "Carlwick... Are you not related to the Dunstons?"

He nodded as he lowered himself back into his seat. "My mother is niece to Lord Dunston via her mother."

"Ah. You're Lord Carlwick's heir?"

Thomas worked to repress a laugh at the catechism. "Nay, lady. I'm his third son. My brother Walter is the heir."

"Aye, I had heard something of that sort. Where did you foster?"

"With the Earl of Pennington, my lady."

She struggled to catch a breath before she could speak. "Good man, the Earl. Have you traveled much lately? Were you on the Continent? Have you met the Black Prince?"

Juliana drew a sharp breath as her mother fired questions at him. "Mother! If you please! Sir Thomas has just arrived. He's tired and has yet to eat his fill. Give him a few moments of rest before you quiz him."

Thomas did laugh out loud this time. Juliana looked shocked, while her mother chuckled. "I can answer your questions quickly, my lady." He looked at the older woman. "I have traveled a great deal lately. I have been on the Continent and have indeed met the Black Prince, but in London, not on the Continent."

The old woman grinned. "Thank you, Sir Thomas." She went on to pepper him with a series of questions about his life, training, thoughts on various subjects, and marital status, stopping only long enough to catch her breath occasionally. Thomas answered them all as courteously as could, deflecting those he didn't wish to say much about. Lady Juliana's discomfort at her mother's brazen curiosity showed in her rising color as he admitted he was a widower, but steered the topic away from the question of how his wife had died.

"And what is your business here with us?" the older lady asked, reaching what he suspected was the true goal of the catechism. "We are of no great importance to the king."

He felt his grin fade. "You are of more importance than you realize. But I believe my business will have to be discussed with Lady Juliana in private. I think, though, it will wait for tomorrow. I've had an exhausting journey and my mind is far from clear."

He feared offending the old lady, but after looking taken aback for a moment, she grinned slyly. "Aye. Of course, Sir Thomas." The suggestive way she said the words made him uneasy, but then she was an elderly, somewhat eccentric, and probably quite ill woman.

She grabbed her cane and hoisted herself to her feet again, emitting a series of creaks from joints in the process. Once upright, she took a moment to catch her breath again. "With your permission, Sir Thomas, I believe I shall retire now. I need my rest."

He stood to acknowledge her. When he sat again, he looked across the table at Lady Juliana. He had expected amusement or the continuation of her exasperation. Instead he saw fear in her eyes.

She masked it quickly when she realized he looked her way, putting on a show of rueful amusement. "Please forgive my mother, Sir Thomas. She means well, truly, though her manner is somewhat forward."

"There's naught to apologize for, my lady. Mothers are allowed much by virtue of the lifetime of sacrifice and care they give their children. Are you her only child, since she lives with you now?"

"Aye. I had an older brother, who died young, and several other brothers and sisters who died at birth." The lady's expression softened in sympathy and love. "She has suffered much. And now her body is failing and she suffers with that. Yet never does she voice any complaint."

A manservant approached and waited for her attention. Lady Juliana nodded to him and the man drew close and leaned over to say something to her, speaking so low only she could hear. After a moment, she nodded. The servant withdrew a bit, though he waited nearby, and she looked back at him.

"Your quarters are ready for you, if you wish to retire, Sir Thomas."

He'd stopped eating a few minutes past. His full belly combined with the effects of an exhausting journey and the potent ale to bring him to a point of having to expend all his energy to prevent his head from drooping onto the table.

"My lady, I cannot tell you how pleasant is the prospect of sleeping this night in a warm bed. I am more grateful than I can say for your hospitality." He stood, noting with some embarrassment that his own knees creaked as he did so.

"If you'll follow Daniel, he'll show you the way." She nodded toward the waiting servant.

Thomas hoped he wouldn't disgrace himself by tottering or falling over in his exhaustion. He made it to his feet without incident and bowed his goodnights to the lady.

"Good rest and sound sleep find you, Sir Thomas," she returned.

Ralf and Bertram followed behind as they trailed the manservant along a corridor, up a flight of stairs, and then along another corridor.

Exhaustion couldn't account totally for his lack of alertness. Some of it also came simply from not expecting any threat in this place. Only a mixture of instinct and luck kept him from being killed or seriously injured.

The sound of a footstep well behind roused his awareness at some deep level. He was already turning when he recognized a faint clicking noise behind him as the sound of a crossbow bolt being released. He threw himself back and to the side, knocking both Ralf and Bertram into the wall.

The bolt whizzed past him, close enough to tear the sleeve of his shirt at his wrist, just below the edge of his chain mail hauberk, and scrape across the flesh. He noted the sting as he whirled to go after whoever had fired the bolt. The torches were widely spaced in this corridor, leaving several recesses in deep shadow. He went to the one he thought closest to where he'd find the shooter. A door there opened at his touch, but it gave onto a steep stone staircase going down. He raced down the steps, but found no one in sight in the corridor that led off it.

Thomas sighed and gave up. Too many doors offered places the shooter might have ducked into. And clearly his assailant knew the keep far better than he did. He wouldn't find him.

As he neared the top of the steps again, a crowd of excited people met him head-on. Ralf and Bertram led the group. "Are you well, my lord?" Bertram asked.

At the same time, Ralf asked, "Did you find him?"

"Nay," he said, answering the second question first, and added, "I'm well. The bolt merely grazed my wrist. Did someone retrieve it?"

"I have it here, Sir Thomas." The servant who'd led them thus far spoke from behind the group, which parted as all turned to stare at him. The man looked shaken, his eyes very wide, his face pale. He held out the crossbow bolt. Sir Thomas took it from him, then grimaced in disgust. It bore no markings or distinctive shape that would tie it to a specific individual.

A group of ladies, drawn by the commotion, hurried down the hall toward them, a pair of maids, and Lady Juliana herself. She ran ahead of the group when she saw him.

"Sir Thomas, what has happened?" She gasped out the words between panting breaths. She looked down at his sleeve and her breath caught on a sharp gasp. "You're injured!"

He noticed the sting at his wrist again for the first time since he'd taken off after the wielder of the crossbow. A red stain spread on the fabric above.

He shook his head. "It's naught. Just a scratch. I'm more concerned with who fired the bolt. And why?"

Her eyes widened as she looked at his arm then up looked up to meet his gaze. "A bolt? A crossbow bolt? Was fired at you?"

He nodded toward the manservant still holding the bolt on his outstretched hands. "Had I not heard him a moment before he fired, 'tis likely I'd have been killed." He stopped and considered. "Unless 'twas not I that was the target. Yet I cannot imagine why anyone should want to kill Ralf or Bertram or your manservant. In truth, I know not why anyone should be bent on my murder either. Is your household always given to such violence, my lady?"

She sucked in a sharp breath. "Nay, Sir Thomas. I...I know not what to say. I'm beyond words." And for a moment, it appeared she was. "Never before, to my knowledge, has a guest been threatened or harmed within these walls. I'm mortified that it should happen now. May I see it?" She nodded toward the bolt.

He handed it to her. She called one of her ladies, who bore a torch, to move closer to allow her a better look at it. She turned it over in her hands several times before she sighed and gave it to one of her maids. "I see nothing on it to indicate who it may have belonged to. Save that in my chest, Avice."

She turned to Thomas and reached for his sleeve. "A scratch this may be, Sir Thomas, yet does it need cleaning and possibly stitching. In your quarters, please." She signaled the manservant to lead the way again.

"You needn't concern yourself with it, my lady," he said. "I barely feel it. I doubt it needs stitching."

In truth he wasn't so sure, but he did know that the lady's presence was doing things to him he could scarce bear. In her concern for the attack on him, she appeared to have forgotten that she'd removed her overgown. The shift she wore now did little to conceal the curves of her lovely figure. He could see clearly beneath the fabric the outline of her breasts and the darker tips pressing against the fabric. He desperately wanted to reach out and touch them, test whether they were as soft as they looked. She'd removed her cap as well, and her hair hung loose around her face, a fall of thick, glossy brown curls halfway down her back.

She looked smaller this way, and younger, yet the strength of her will and authority forestalled all argument, and he allowed her to accompany them to his quarters without demur.

While Ralf and Bertram helped him remove sword and mail, she sent her maids for water, clean linen, and salve. When he stood in his shirt and breeches, she took his hand and pushed the sleeve up from his bleeding wrist. She used the sleeve to wipe away the blood, promising to have the shirt repaired and laundered.

As he'd told her, the wound was little more than a scratch. He heard her sigh with relief as she realized it as well.

Still she washed it carefully, holding his hand in hers to steady it, then smeared salve across the injury and wound a length of clean linen around the wrist. Her hands shook the entire time, whether from fear, anger, or something else, he couldn't judge.

When she'd finished, she continued to hold his hand a while longer. Her gaze ran up his sleeve and paused a moment at the opening where his partially unlaced shirt showed his chest and throat. Her hand tightened around his, though he was sure she wasn't aware of it. She slowly looked up from his throat to his jaw, his mouth and then met his eyes.

He stared back at her, meeting the blaze that lit her light, greenish eyes. There was much more within this calm, sweet-seeming lady than could be read on the surface. Deep, raging emotions boiled inside her, held in check by her strong will. Among them, he was sure, was a passion she just barely contained. And his presence roused it in her. Her eyes widened. Moist, glistening lips parted.

How could Lord Groswick leave a lady such as this alone for so long a time? She was so lovely, so warm and welcoming. It raised a deep anger and even deeper doubt in him. A man surely wouldn't leave the side of such a lady for any length of time without desperate reason. Were she his, it would take some truly grave need to force him from her for more than a few days.

His men must have put more wood on the fire. His body was blazing. The warmth gathered and settled in his groin, making him hard and needy. He dared not let it show and fought with all his will to contain the raging inferno that fired his blood.

The lady abruptly realized the danger. She closed her eyes, lowered her head, and took a deep, noisy breath. Her breasts bounced as she let the air stream out again. It took her a moment to get control, but then she opened her eyes and released his hand.

"Sir Thomas, I apologize. None of this should have happened." She rose to her feet. "Every measure will be taken to discover the culprit and ensure he's punished."

He suspected her apology was intended to cover more than just his injury.

"I trust you will, my lady."

Chapter Two

Her skin was petal-soft where it pressed on his. Her breath fluttered softly against his throat, while her bare breasts skimmed his chest. He reached out to put his arms around her slim shoulders and draw her closer against him.

She made a sound like a hoarse kitten's purring as he pressed a line of kisses up along her throat to the underside of her jaw. He rubbed up and down her spine and she shivered in response.

Her lips were moist and soft against his, fluttering gently at first as he sucked and nipped at them, then parting to let his tongue invade the sweet recesses of her mouth. His hard, full cock pressed into her belly.

He wanted her so badly he ached all over with it. A sheen of sweat slicked his body as he moved against her. Her breasts were springy comforting mounds – small, pleasant handfuls in his palms. The tips beaded hard when his questing fingers searched and tweaked them. Her moan reverberated against his body, sinking in, setting his blood on fire in his veins.

He rolled over, taking her along, so that she ended up below him. He kissed her brow, her cheeks, her jaw, and down her throat to her breasts. The tips were sweet and hard against his swirling tongue. She squirmed and panted beneath him.

He brushed a hand down her belly and into her cleft. Fingering the folds there, he found the damp proof of her readiness.

Her legs parted easily when he shifted her. The tip of his cock found the entrance. A quick push and he was in. Hot, hot,

hot, tight, damp, and sweet. He began to pump in and out. The walls of her tunnel tightened against him, trying to hold him within.

He pushed forward again....

"Sir Thomas. Sir Thomas!"

He rolled over and let go the dream with an irritated grunt.

Ralf stood over him, wearing a worried frown. "Are you well, Sir Thomas? You were moaning and groaning in your sleep, and we feared your injury pained you."

He pushed hair off his face and rubbed his eyes. "No pain. I dreamt. What is the hour?"

"Just past dawn, Sir Thomas."

Time to rise and be about the business of the day. A part of him longed to roll over and sink into the dream again. "A moment. Give me a moment."

The young man nodded and backed away until Thomas indicated he was ready to dress.

On his way to the great hall, he realized he felt less than rested, though he'd certainly enjoyed being in a real bed for the first time in days. The scratch on his wrist burned faintly but it hadn't kept him from sleep.

He found platters laden with bread and fruit set out in the great hall and sat to it gratefully, again noting the good order and management of the keep. Servants appeared, bringing more food and drink. One stopped near his seat, hesitated, and leaned over to ask, "Is there anything more I might bring you, my lord?"

When Sir Thomas turned toward him, the man drew back sharply, almost as though he feared a blow or other reprisal.

"The cider in the pitcher is low," he said. "You might bring some more."

"Aye, my lord." The man snatched up the pitcher.

Sir Thomas tried to puzzle out the odd expression on the man's face. Not fear, exactly, but worry and suspicion creased his brow and carved deep lines around his eyes. It looked like more suspicion than an unknown and unexpected guest should deserve.

He didn't see Lady Juliana during the meal, though various people came and went while he ate. When he was done, he asked a passing servant where he might find her.

"I believe she's in the storeroom with the steward, my lord," the man answered. "I can show you the way if it suits you."

"It does."

He followed the man along a couple of long corridors, past doors that led off to various parts of the keep, around a sharp bend, and down a short flight of stairs. The storeroom was a large, dim, and gloomy room, lined on one side with rough shelves, and on the other with barrels and racks.

They followed the sound of voices, weaving around wooden bins and crates, stepping over sacks lying near some of the barrels, and skirting a huge vat that took up nearly half the width the room. They found Lady Juliana at the far end, consulting with a man of middle years who held a list and a charcoal marker.

Lady Juliana and the man looked up at the sound of footsteps approaching.

For a brief moment before she controlled it, a glow of sheer welcome and pleasure lit her face. It passed too quickly to do more than make his pulse jump, but he knew that a longer look like that would warm him all the way down to his toes.

Then the flash of delight was gone, and her expression showed nothing but polite interest. "Sir Thomas. I trust you rested well this past night? Your wound didn't pain you overmuch?"

"It did not, and I rested well enough, thank you, my lady. I see you are busy, but I hope you might have a few minutes to spare me. There are matters I must discuss with you in private."

Worry creased her pretty brow for a moment, but then she relaxed her expression. "Of course." She turned to the other man, the steward, he presumed. "You'll talk with the miller about that allotment again?"

"Aye, my lady," he answered. "I'll go myself this afternoon."

The steward stared hard at him, a wary, almost fearful look. For a household run by a gentle, seemingly sweet-natured lady, there seemed to be a great deal of that going around. Yet the man's expression had been much milder while dealing with the lady herself.

"Thank you." She turned and began to walk away, stopped, and waited for him. "If you'll come with me, Sir Thomas?"

He followed her from the room and back along the endless-seeming corridor. "We'll go to the room my lord used as his office. I've taken it for my own purposes as I see to things in his absence."

"He's been gone for some time now, has he not?" Thomas asked as they traversed the hall.

"Aye. Nigh on a year."

"You don't find running the keep and the demesne too large a burden?"

At first he wasn't sure she'd heard. It took her a moment to answer. "Nay. Well, aye, at times, it is a burden. But someone must do it, and I am the lady. All look to me for their well-being and protection." She drew a deep breath and blew it out slowly. "'Tis a great deal of responsibility." Juliana stopped in front of a closed door, pushed down the latch, and opened it. When he was inside, she nudged it shut again. "We can be private here, my lord."

The room was small but comfortable. The morning sunlight shone in through a window on his right, adding extra warmth to a space already heated by a low fire on the left. A table, a set of shelves, a cabinet with drawers and two chairs furnished the space. Each of the chairs bore a stuffed cushion, though those were the only feminine touches in an otherwise plain and businesslike space.

"Have a seat, if you will, Sir Thomas," she said.

"If *you* will, my lady."

She smiled. "I should prefer to stand right now. I like to move around when I need to think."

Or when you're nervous. He didn't say it aloud, but the lady was clearly worried, and he didn't think that was due solely to being closed in a room with a man she barely knew and was too aware of. Did she fear the news he might be bringing about her husband?

He nodded acknowledgement and remained on his feet as well. "You've no doubt guessed I've come to ask about your husband. The king is concerned about him, as we've had no word of his whereabouts for nigh on a year."

"He is fighting with the Prince on the Continent, Sir Thomas, though I've had no word from him either and cannot say anything more of his exact location."

Sir Thomas drew a deep breath. "My lady, please forgive me if this discomposes you unduly, but I fear no one knows where he is or what he is now doing."

She gave him a quick, panic-stricken look and turned to face the window. "Is he not with the Prince in France?"

"The Prince is back in London, my lady. And Lord Groswick was not with him. In fact, the Prince has not seen him at any time, either on the Continent or here. He has no knowledge of his location. The king was concerned that one of his barons should disappear thus and asked me to investigate the matter."

Without moving her gaze from the scene outside the window, she reached out for the back of the chair nearby. Her palm slipped off and nearly unbalanced her, but she didn't turn around. She reached again and found the top edge. Before she clenched her fingers on it, he saw that her hand trembled.

"He did not join the Prince in France?" Her voice sounded thin and strained.

"Nay, my lady."

"And there's been no word at all from him?"

"Save you've received some message from him, nay."

"I have not." The words came out on a sigh.

"Have you had any word at all from him since he left the keep last year?"

She shook her head. "Nay."

"Know you how many men rode with him when he left here?"

For a moment she didn't answer. "Some twenty, I believe. He was to meet others along the way."

"Have you asked if any other families heard from others who went?"

"I've inquired. No one has heard anything."

"Why did you not send word to the king? Surely a year is a very long time to go with no message?"

Her fingers tightened on the chair. "Sir Thomas, had you known my husband, you would not think it so strange. He was a man of few words at the best of times."

"But to go a year…"

"'Tis not inconceivable."

The silence that followed was not comfortable. He hoped she would expand on why she thought her husband would remain silent, would even remain apart for so long from a wife as lovely and sweet as herself. She did not add anything, however.

"Lady Juliana… I know not how to ask this delicately. How well did you know your husband?"

That brought her whirling around to face him. Some of the color had drained from her face, but there was also a look of fear, almost panic, in her eyes. She controlled it with an effort and made herself smile. The expression curved her mouth but left the rest of her face unmoved. "How well do most wives know their husbands? Perhaps they know them well after many years of living and working together, but I had only three years with my lord before he left. I knew the surface well enough and little of what was beneath."

"Did he ever give you reason to believe—or even think—he might be doing something other than going to battle?"

Her eyes unfocused for a moment as she thought. "Nay, I cannot remember him giving any such indication." She threaded her fingers together in agitation. "What shall we do? Have you talked to his uncle, the Earl of Everham? Perhaps he spent time there?"

"I spoke to him in London," Thomas said. "He knows no more of his nephew than do we."

She was starting to lose the struggle to control her expression. "I don't... What enquiries will you make now?"

He rubbed the back of his neck, wondering how his shoulder muscles could have gotten so tight so early in the day. "With your permission, I would speak to some of your people here. Perhaps someone heard a stray word that might give us a clue. I'd like also to speak to your crofters. Already I have spoken with many who live along the way from here to the sea, seeking someone who might have remembered seeing his party, but I have turned up naught. Not a one admits to knowing anything about them, or even recalls seeing him or his company go by."

"Does that not seem passing strange to you, Sir Thomas?"

"It does, my lady. Can you think of any reason why he might want to hide or disappear?"

Juliana shut her eyes for a moment. When she opened them she shook her head. "Nay. No reason."

"Did he not have enemies?"

She thought for a moment. "A few. I don't believe that any of those would have the nerve to attack him, save possibly from an ambush." Her sharp glance speared through him. "Sir Thomas…" She struggled to get the words out. "Do you think my husband yet lives?"

He stared at her, studying her expression. She had already more than half accepted that her husband was gone. She must have begun to wonder if it were so after so long a time of silence, but perhaps she did not want to believe. With him echoing her own suspicions, she could no longer avoid the likelihood of her husband's death. He could not read how she felt about that, other than that it left her afraid. The fear was natural and not surprising, for if Lord Groswick were dead, it put her future in grave doubt. It was his turn to find difficulty in speaking.

"Lady, you seem to be one who believes in plain words and open thoughts. I hope it is a courtesy I grant when I speak plainly in return. I do not believe your husband walks this Earth anymore, though I cannot begin to guess the method or location of his passing."

"Oh." The series of hard breaths that followed that small exclamation weren't quite sobs, but perhaps a shortness brought on by strong emotion. "Might he have been captured by enemies on the Continent?"

Thomas shook his head. "We would surely have heard. A baron is too valuable a pawn. There would have been a demand for ransom or exchange of prisoners."

"But then what could have happened?"

"An ambush, as you mentioned, is a possibility. Perhaps he was beset by robbers or brigands."

She nodded and rubbed her brow with a hand that shook. "What am I to do now?"

Her distress called to him. Without thinking or willing it, he moved toward her. "Lady Juliana. The king will see no harm comes to you. Should it be shown your husband is dead, the king will appoint a new lord for the lands and keep, but I'll have a word with him and request he have a care for you as well."

She didn't answer. Her thoughts seemed focused inward, and her fingers knotted together. She'd been carrying much responsibility and clearly doing it well, but he suspected this was a blow that could make the burden much greater. She braced herself on a long, hard inhalation. "I've managed heretofore. I shall continue to do so."

Sunlight coming in the window gleamed on a few dark brown curls that escaped from beneath her cap. It seemed to play around her slender, graceful form—such a slight figure to carry all the burdens she now bore. He couldn't help but admire her. She was just such a lady as he would want for himself.

A most unworthy thought crossed his mind. If Groswick were truly dead, the lady was free to marry again. All he'd learned inclined him to believe it was so. But should he harbor a hope that it was?

He dared lay a hand on her shoulder. The warmth of her body seeped through her gown and sent a jolt of heat into him that sped through his veins. "You've managed well, my lady. Extremely well from what I've seen of your keep and demesne. All is in good order."

She looked up at him. Her troubled expression lightened but didn't disappear. "I thank you, Sir Thomas. I find one does what one has to, whether one wishes to or not. I did not ask for this burden, but having had it laid on me, I could not fail to take it up and meet its demands to the best of my ability."

"It appears your ability is considerable."

"In truth, I must admit that my mother has been a great help in it. She has a prodigious ability for organizing and managing affairs."

"'Tis well you have help. But my lady, once the king hears that Groswick is presumed dead, he will provide you with further assistance. Had Groswick any heirs?"

A flash of pain made her eyes narrow for a moment before she controlled it. "We had no children." That no doubt accounted for some of the sadness that sometimes showed in her expression. "As for other heirs, I think not. I've been told he had only one other brother, who died young. I suppose the Earl, his uncle, would have some claim. I know of no one else."

"'Twill be for the king to decide then."

She nodded and drew a deep breath. "Aye."

"What have you of dower lands?"

"None, my lord."

"None?"

"My Lord Groswick felt there was no need of it."

He stared at her, stunned. "That was not well done. And not customary, either. Know you why he felt so?"

She said nothing for a moment, and he had the impression she was deciding how to reply. "Nay." The word carried little conviction, however.

Here was a mystery. The lady knew or had some idea why her husband had chosen not to dower her, but she didn't want to say what it was. He could think of few reasons a husband would act so, and none that seemed to apply. The lady was nobly born herself, apparently unlanded otherwise, and gave no indication of being unstable or unreliable. It did go some way to explain why the death of her husband should cause her so much fear.

He leaned a little closer to her, meaning only to give reassurance. "You worry that a new lord will come in and you'll have no place. Fear not, my lady. When I report to the king, I'll mention your predicament and ensure that provision is made for you."

The smile that spread across her face was surprised, sad, hopeful, and grateful, all at once. He was stunned himself, when she suddenly rushed forward and wrapped her arms around him, chest against his, resting her face on his shoulder. She squeezed tightly. His body reacted. Heat poured through him, gathering in his groin, hardening his cock. She felt like an angel in his arms, and he wanted to hold her against him until he couldn't stand it anymore, then bury himself in her.

That way lay danger, his conscience reminded him. Her husband was likely dead, but until they knew, he had no right to think of her in those terms.

It took an effort that left him sweating and shaking, but he finally forced himself to disengage from the lady. At his gentle pressure on her arms, she backed up, her expression suddenly horrified. She looked up at him with tears in her eyes.

"Sir Thomas, I do apologize. I had no right...I know not what I was thinking. Truly, I am not normally so...forward."

"I do not think so, my lady. You were overcome with the emotion of the moment. Think no more of it."

The heat and pressure refused to go away so long as he looked at her. He needed to get out before he disgraced himself.

"My lady, if you'll excuse me, I have things to do and I know you do as well. Do you object if I question members of your household concerning Lord Groswick?"

"Nay, Sir Thomas. Do as...you will." Her voice wobbled and broke.

"Thank you. Lady Juliana." He bowed to her, turned, and left.

* * * * *

Thomas had wanted to question the bailiff, but when he inquired about it, he was told the man was out on business with some of the crofters. He asked about the steward and learned he, too, had departed on an errand. He recalled that Juliana had asked him to do something for her that morning.

He shrugged and went to the kitchens, where the head cook ungraciously consented to answer his questions, so long as he could continue to stir the pot he leaned over while he did so. The man identified himself as John Cookson.

"You've been here how many years, John Cookson?" Thomas asked.

"All my life, my lord," the man answered. "My father was head cook here before me."

"You knew Lord Groswick well enough then?"

The man shrugged. "How well does a cook know the lord of the keep?"

"Usually very well indeed, though not necessarily from personal contact," Thomas suggested.

The man looked up from his pot. The words had surprised a small grin from him, though it faded quickly. "Ah well, you have the right of that. I knew my lord well enough in that way."

"And what sort of man would you say he was?"

John looked back down into his pot and stirred thoughtfully for a moment before he answered. "A hard lord. He was raised with no softness, though being the only son of his father, he grew to expect he could have aught that he wished. A man with no gentleness in him, though as to that, I suppose 'tis not so different from most other lords." The cook slanted him a suspicious look from narrowed eyes.

"Would you say he was a fair lord?"

Again the thoughtful pause ensued. "As to that, I cannot truly judge."

An interesting reply, Thomas thought. "Lady Juliana tells me Lord Groswick has been gone over a year now, with no word from him. Does that seem strange to you?"

The answer took long enough in coming. Thomas began to wonder if the man was habitually so slow to speak. If not, then was it his presence or the subject matter making him so uncomfortable?

"Nay, not so strange. My lord's will was his own, and he looked to no one else's needs, wants, or pleasure in his actions. He would not likely have felt he must send messages or word of his plans here. He'd not have thought of it, save that he needed something from us."

"Did you know anything of his plans when he left?"

The man stopped stirring for a moment and drew a deep breath. "I believe he was to meet the Prince on the Continent, my lord."

"You heard no whisper that their true destination might be some other place. Or that they planned a stop somewhere?"

The man shook his head. "Nay."

"How many rode out with him?"

The hand holding the spoon showed a slight tremor. "I know not that I can recall with any accuracy. Perhaps two dozen."

"Did you know those who rode out with him?"

John turned a look on him that showed distress and worry. "Nay, my lord. That is…" He paused and took a breath. "They were my lord's foster brothers or mercenaries who attached themselves. I knew them not at all well."

"So you wouldn't know if the men's families had heard any word from them?"

"Nay, my lord." The man let out a breath in a sigh that sounded relieved. Thomas wondered what question he had feared would be asked.

"Know you the names of those men?"

John stiffened and drew a sharp breath. "Sir Robert of… I know not where, my lord. There was a Sir Wilfred and Lord Adam of…Exeter, was it? Forgive me, my lord, but I am poor with names."

So poor he couldn't give a single name specific enough to let him trace the person. But then the man was a cook. He had no reason to be concerned with the names of noble visitors, save that they were normally the subject of much gossip.

Thomas sighed himself. "Thank you for your help, John." He started to leave, then stopped and turned around as thought of another question. "Lady Juliana and Lord Groswick were wed near three years past. How did Lord Groswick feel about the lady?"

"My lord!" John said sharply. "'Tis not my place to talk about my lord and his lady that way." He drew a couple of breaths. "But you know Lady Juliana. She is a lady both sweet and wise beyond her years. How could anyone fail to love her?"

"How indeed?" he asked. Thomas thanked the man and took his leave.

He stopped to ask a young man passing by if he knew where the housekeeper might be found and followed the directions given. On the way he mused that this might be the oddest keep he'd ever been in.

Chapter Three

Juliana made it through her remaining morning chores. She only dropped one cup, shattering it, a piece of marking charcoal in the main storeroom, and a loaf of bread in the kitchen. Not bad, she decided, considering how badly she was shaking. Just after midday, she talked to John, the head cook, concerning food plans for the next few days, and managed it with only a slight tremor or two.

Unfortunately, the cook, a grizzled older man with thick body and huge hands, noticed her shaken condition.

"My lady, forgive my impertinence, but is all well with you?" he asked.

"Aye, of course."

The man nodded. "I feared that Sir Thomas's arrival might have discomposed you. He is asking questions."

She drew a deep breath. "Aye, I know."

"He asked a number of questions about my lord and his men. He also asked about yourself and Lord Groswick and how he regarded you. None here will betray you, my lady."

"I know that. And I do appreciate your loyalty, considering that I am not native here."

The cook's homely face broke into a grin. "Ye may not have been born here, my lady, but it has been clear since shortly after you arrived that ye belonged here."

Remembering her husband's treatment of her, Juliana sighed. "Clear, perhaps, to some, but certainly not all."

"Now, my lady, fret ye not. All will be well."

She summoned a smile for his benefit. "I thank you, John."

When she stopped briefly in the great hall for a midday meal, she learned that Sir Thomas had questioned several of the household staff about Lord Groswick. The two who spoke to her directly stressed that they'd said nothing to him beyond the fact that their lord had left some time ago and they'd heard nothing from him since.

By the time she returned to her solar for a quick afternoon rest, her nerves were strung tight. Finding someone already waiting for her there didn't improve her state of mind.

"Mother?"

Lady Ardsley rose from the bench where she'd been resting. "You spoke with Sir Thomas earlier. What does he know?"

"He knows little, but he suspects much. He knows Groswick didn't meet the Prince in France, and he's been able to find no evidence that he ever made the journey. He seems to have checked quite thoroughly."

"Tell me all."

Juliana related as much as she could remember of her conversation and also told her what John had said about the questions Sir Thomas asked him. The longer she spoke, the more agitated her mother became. She stood and paced up and down the room. "He's no fool, this Sir Thomas. And he seems quite determined as well." She stopped and turned to Juliana. "He could be dangerous."

"He is dangerous. In more ways than just the one."

Her mother gave her a hard stare. Juliana loved her mother, but she had also grown in understanding of her over the past few years. The mind within the wizened figure, hidden by her charming, sometimes silly, chatty manner, was both sharp and calculating. Juliana wondered what scheme she was hatching now. Even at that, she wasn't prepared for what her mother said next.

"You'll have to seduce him."

"What? Mother! What in heaven do you mean?"

"What I said. Come, Juliana, you're no child anymore. You know what it means to seduce a man."

"I know what it means, though I know not why you think I'm capable of such a thing."

"Every woman is capable of it, but your beauty makes you more capable than most."

She shook that off. Whatever beauty she might possess had had little influence on Lord Groswick. And now her face bore ugly scars as a result.

"I know not how I would go about it."

"I can tell you. Men have their weaknesses. And it seems Sir Thomas has been celibate for some time, which will make him more susceptible yet. I cannot think a man such as he finds that easy." The older woman sighed. "I've seen him watch you, as well. He's drawn to you whether he wants it so or not."

"But, mother! Why would I do such a thing? What can it gain me?"

Her mother paused and started pacing again. "He's going to learn... He's too intelligent and too persistent. He already suspects something is amiss. I think he's already wondering if Groswick actually left the keep at all. He's mentioned being unable to find anyone who saw his party pass on the road. If he doesn't already wonder, he will shortly when he finds no one in the vicinity admits to seeing him. Or if they do, their stories may not match." Her mother drew a deep breath, paused in her pacing, and lifted her head to look at Juliana again. "I fear for you. He's a hard man. I fear there's little mercy in him."

The familiar fear washed over her, but she tried to deny it. "He's an honorable man. He'd understand if we explained the circumstances."

"We cannot depend on that. You must tie him to you in a stronger way. He'll be much less likely to denounce a woman he's lain with."

"Denounce…"

"We've known all along how the world would view what happened, though none who know you and Groswick would question it."

Juliana sighed. She hated the lies with all her soul. The fact that so many others were imperiling their souls in the same way on her behalf tore her conscience to shreds at times. And Sir Thomas had seemed so kind and understanding. "Perhaps I should just tell him…"

"Nay!" Her mother turned sharply to face her. "You'll do no such thing." Her always pale face grew even whiter, and she appeared to waver.

Juliana helped her to a chair. "I don't like the lies and the deception, Mother. I fear it may cause more serious harm."

"I've told all that no harm is to be done to Sir Thomas or his men. There should be…no repeat of the…crossbow episode." Lady Ardsley struggled with her breath again.

"Have you learned who did it?"

"Nay, though I'd guess 'twas Peter Randolph. You know how he idolizes you."

The bailiff's son had adored her from the moment she'd arrived. "Aye. He is my guess as well. I'll have a word with him."

Her mother nodded. "You must do something to bind Sir Thomas as well. He's too great a danger to you."

"I cannot believe you truly want me to seduce him. He'll resist it. He still sees me as a married woman, and to lay with me would be adultery. I think he'll not want that on his conscience." She sighed. "I don't want it on my conscience that I led him into that sin. Though why I should now get so nice with my conscience I know not. There are enough stains on it already."

Her mother stood and came over to pat her shoulder. "Nay, Juliana. What happened was an accident. You bear no responsibility for it. Only Groswick can be blamed."

"How does one blame a man who is dead?"

"One doesn't. Nor does one blame oneself for the accident that killed him."

"If we hadn't argued, though, and I hadn't tried to push him away from me…"

"He might have killed you instead. Of the two of you, the world is better with you still in it and him not, rather than the other way round."

"It matters little. Sir Thomas will not be able to prove anything in any case."

"Nonetheless, the more we can do to minimize the risk, the better."

"What would you have me do, Mother? I was unable to rouse my husband. I see no reason why I should be able to seduce Sir Thomas."

"I've seen him look at you with the heat of desire in his eyes," her mother answered. "A heat I never saw in Groswick's. Not for you, nor for any other woman. He was not a man for women."

Her mother began pacing again. After a moment of that, she said, "Offer him a bath tonight. He'll surely take the offer. And, of course, as the lady of the household, 'twill be your duty to assist him. You'll rouse him. He has noticed you, Juliana. I saw the way he looked at you. And, truly, how great a burden can it be? He's a comely man and appears to be an honorable one. He treats courteously all who cross his path."

"I do believe him an honorable man. And therein lies the problem. I dislike to have it on my conscience that I lured him into an act he'll consider dishonorable."

"You must protect yourself as much as possible, Juliana. For my sake, if for no other. What would I do without you? I'm an old woman with little more life left, but I'll leave it more happily knowing your future is secure."

"Mother..." Juliana sighed, knowing her mother had found the one sure way to win her compliance. "So be it. Tell me what I must do."

Chapter Four

Dinner that evening was a more festive affair then usual. Juliana had planned with the cook to serve a more bountiful variety of foods at the meal, in honor of Sir Thomas's presence. Fortunately, with the harvest just behind them, supplies were plentiful. She made sure as well that servants would keep the pitchers of wine full and cups refilled quickly.

The best gown she owned was the one in which she'd been married to Lord Groswick, but she couldn't bear the thought of putting it on again. Her second-best gown was still a grand enough affair, with long, flowing sleeves in deep rose velvet, worn over a shift with green embroidery at the bosom and hem. The color suited her.

Thomas's reaction when she entered the hall was all she could have hoped for. His expression had been somewhere between neutral and a frown as he talked to William Randolph, the bailiff, but it changed to astonishment and wonder when he turned and caught sight of her.

She heard others commenting, but all her attention centered on Sir Thomas. It pleased her that he was so very different from Groswick in looks. His sky blue eyes could be hard and compelling, but they could also sparkle with amusement or shine with admiration, as they did now. They were so very unlike Groswick's impenetrably dark eyes which never seemed to show any emotion other than disdain or anger. And Sir Thomas's very light blond hair reminded her of the angels on the tapestries in the chapel. Not that anything else about the man was so ethereal, however. He had a solid presence one could not ignore when he was in the same room. Still, she wanted to touch his hair, to see if it was as soft as it looked.

When their gazes met, she felt the same strange sense of connection and sharing she'd had yesterday when she'd first seen him. It was almost as though he could reach inside her and draw out something she barely knew existed, or something that existed only because he was there. That strange and different sensation made her feel a bit shaky with a combination of fear and excitement.

"My lady, you look splendid tonight," Thomas said. "How any man could bring himself to leave you after setting eyes on your loveliness, I cannot imagine."

"You flatter me, my lord." She couldn't hold his gaze and dropped her eyes.

"May I escort you to your seat?"

She nodded and placed her hand on the arm he offered. A surge of tingling warmth spread through her fingers and up her arm, into the rest of her body, from the spot where her hand lay on the fabric of his sleeve. When he moved, she felt the flex of hard muscle under the linen.

It was difficult to break the connection when they arrived at their seats. She'd never wanted to cling to anyone other than her mother, but she had to fight a desire to put her hand back on his arm and try to hold onto him.

He placed her in her usual spot at the left side of the center chair. She swept an arm out to invite him to take the lord's place. As he was the only member of the nobility present other than herself and her mother, courtesy demanded he have that seat. Her own desires accorded with the requirement.

Dinner went smoothly, with the courses arriving in good order, and well-cooked, as they always were. She watched the servants refill Sir Thomas's wine cup several times. She drank somewhat more than she normally would herself, but it helped steady her nerves for what lay ahead. A group of servants performed musical numbers they'd practiced as entertainment after dinner. They were in fine voice and, apparently inspired by the presence of guests, outdid themselves in both enthusiasm and melody.

As the meal concluded, before he could tell her he was ready to bid her goodnight, she turned to him and said, "I've had a bath prepared for you, my lord. I regret we had not the time to provide one last night, but we'll make up the lack this night."

"And will you assist me, my lady?" he asked.

He was making this almost too easy. "Of course, my lord. 'Tis both my duty and a pleasure in this instance."

His smile transfigured his face, making it the most beautiful thing she'd ever seen. It made her breath hitch in her chest and her heart pound harder. When he stood, she did as well.

"If you'll retire to your quarters, my lord, you'll find the bath awaits. Leave the door unbarred and I'll join you in a moment." She held up an arm and let the wide sleeve swing free. "This is not the best choice to wear while bathing a guest."

"Nay. Dress more comfortably, and I'll await your attentions." He bowed to her, then to everyone in the hall, and left.

Juliana hurried to her quarters, where she found her mother waiting for her, along with her maid.

"The bath has been prepared for him," Lady Ardsley announced as her maid helped Juliana out of the velvet overgown.

"Mother, are you well?" Juliana asked, noting how very pale her mother was and the way her hands shook even more than usual.

"Well enough, my love. Today has not been one of my better days."

That was as close as Lady Ardsley would come to admitting she was in considerable pain.

"Go to your bed," Juliana directed, then looked at the maid. "Avice, settle my mother, and then fetch some of the pain tincture from the herb room for her."

Normally her mother protested vehemently against taking the medicine which tasted foul and left her feeling dizzy afterward, though it did help her sleep on her bad days. It was some measure of her condition that she made no demurral.

The maid nodded. Her mother stopped as she was leaving and came back to give Juliana a spasmodic hug. Then, as though embarrassed by the display of emotion, she turned and left as fast as she was able.

Juliana watched her go, put a light wrapper over her shift, and went down the hall to Sir Thomas's solar. As promised, the door was unbarred.

She peeked in. The tub sat near the fireplace in the spacious solar allotted to important guests, and Sir Thomas sat in it. His back was to her, his blond head resting on the side. "Come in, Lady Juliana," he called, without turning around to verify her identity. "I sent my squire and my man out for a while."

She drew a deep breath and moved into the room, searching for the towels and soap the servants should have left. She found them on a stool beside the tub. It took all her courage to turn around and face him.

He wasn't as relaxed as he wanted her to think. Though his head tilted back, apparently at rest, his eyes were narrowed and watched her intently. His arms lay along the sides of the tub, but his fingers clutched at the edge with more force than needed to keep him steady.

She didn't want to stare at him, but could hardly restrain herself. He was the most beautiful man she'd ever seen. She'd known it from the moment she first looked up in the great hall and met his gaze, but seeing him now, stripped down to his skin and the essence of his being, she understood better.

This was a man who did not need the outer trappings of knighthood and good birth to impress. Confidence rode his shoulders like a cloak, and nobility radiated from him in a halo echoed by his golden-blond hair.

At the same time there was something utterly sensual about him as well. His skin was firm and sleek over hard muscle. It almost begged her to touch it. A light pelt of blond hair covered the center of his chest, narrowing toward his waist. God had indeed created a creature of near-perfection in this man, and that in itself, was enough to make her wonder about her course. But she'd promised her mother.

Juliana moved the stool closer to the tub, set the towels aside and sat down. She rubbed soap on a cloth and reached over to wash his shoulder. "I hope you'll forgive me if I'm somewhat awkward at this, Sir Thomas. I've had few occasions to practice. You'll tell me if I do something that...bothers you."

His mouth crooked into a wry grin. "I expect you'll do any number of things that will bother me, but I'll tell you if any are unbearable."

"My lord—!"

"Nay, my lady, forgive me. I'm teasing you."

She breathed out a sigh and relaxed a little as she washed his hand. "Of course."

"Did you not do this for your husband from time to time?"

"Aye, though not so often as all that. In general, he preferred to bathe alone. Or with only his manservants attending him."

"Forgive me for speaking ill of the man, but I cannot admire his taste or intelligence if he chose to have manservants attending him over yourself."

Juliana shrugged and ran the cloth up and down his arm, then switched to his other shoulder. "'Twas his choice. He valued his privacy."

"Ah. I suppose I can understand that."

Desperate to change the subject, Juliana asked, "But what about yourself, my lord? 'Tis strange that a man so noble and courteous and handsome as yourself has not wed again." She stumbled on seeing the way his expression darkened. "Or I presume you're not wed. Did you not say—? Am I wrong?"

His frown was very grim. "I am not married. My one experience with it did not encourage me to embark on the journey again."

Juliana hesitated. "You still grieve for her."

He remained silent for some time. Just when she'd concluded he wouldn't answer, he said, "I do not grieve for her. She wasn't worth a single tear."

After a start of astonishment, Juliana leaned over him to wash his other arm, and was treated to the scent of his body, his essential manly smell. Her breasts were dangerously close to his chest. If she looked down, she could see…Yes, the parts of him normally hidden beneath his clothes were just as impressive as what showed.

She felt the heat rising in her face when she realized he knew what she saw. That knowledge mixed with the hard anger still showing in his expression.

"Not worth a tear?" she asked " Surely the loss of any human being is worth at least some grief, no matter how much they might have hurt us."

He softened a bit. "You take on so much responsibility, 'tis easy to forget how young you still are," he said.

"I'm one and twenty," she protested. "Not so very young."

"To an old man of near thirty, you seem like a mere child."

She most definitely did not want him thinking of her as a child. "You tease again, my lord. You are no old man."

"Perhaps less so in body than in spirit. I've traveled too much, seen too much of battle and other evils of this world. I'm weary of it. Perhaps it's your innocence of spirit that makes you seem so young."

She carefully cleaned his right hand, working the cloth between his fingers and over his palm. "Do not impute too much virtue to me, my lord. I have sinned. I have sinned grievously, in truth."

She drew back. He raised a leg to allow her easy access for cleaning it. Juliana rubbed more soap into the cloth and set to work on his foot.

"The Bible and the church say we are all sinners," he answered. "But some sin more and more vilely than others."

The answer would surely dismay her, possibly even hurt, but she asked anyway. "What did your wife do to hurt you so much?"

Muscles tensed in hard bunches in his calf as she washed it.

"She lied and betrayed me. She tore my family apart and estranged me from them."

Juliana struggled to control her reaction when she heard the word "lied." Her conscience, always bitterly ready to reproach her, roused and nagged at her. She had little family — only her mother — but it had saved her at a time when she might have found it difficult to survive otherwise. She hated for him that he was estranged from his. "I am sorry. It must have been terrible for you."

He shrugged but remained tense, even as she washed his foot and asked him to change legs. "I survived. She did not. I know not if that was God's justice or mercy."

"How did she die?"

"Giving birth. The child did not survive either. Though I buried him as my son, he was not." His tone admitted no grief but still she could feel the pain he would not voice. It hurt her on his behalf.

"Ah. She was unfaithful to you, then? 'Tis hard to believe, though, that a woman would not keep faith with someone like yourself."

He laughed harshly, a sound that held a world of irony, but no amusement. "I suppose she kept faith in her way, though I could not prove it, after she'd achieved her desires and cost me much of what I held dear."

She looked up from the knee she stroked with the cloth. "My lord? I fear you speak in riddles."

His smile held the same twisted irony. "Ah, well. It has been said that I'm no easy man to understand. In this, though, 'tis not that it's difficult, so much as I find it difficult to speak of."

"You needn't then, if you find it so painful." Juliana put more soap on the rag and handed it to him when she stood up. "If you would wash yourself, my lord, I'll begin on your hair." She nodded toward his privates and he took her meaning as well as accepting the cloth from her.

"'Tis an old wound, and should not be so painful now as it was." He was quiet a moment while she dipped water in a tin cup and poured it over his head to wet his hair. "Margaret was betrothed to my brother. Not Carlwick, but my next older brother. She was a beautiful but willful young woman, charming and spoiled. Accustomed to having her own way. I believe her parents never denied her aught that she wanted if it were in their power to give it to her. When she came to our home for the betrothal to my brother, she looked at us all and decided that she wanted myself rather than Edwin."

He sighed as she massaged the soap into his hair and relaxed somewhat. "I cannot entirely fault her for that. Edwin is...slow in wit and not much to look upon in truth, though he has a warm and loving heart. But the arrangement was long made and 'twas her duty to honor it."

"She did not?"

"She did all in her power to get out of it. She begged, pleaded, wept, moaned, even attempted to starve herself. That did not last long. She had not the will to resist food for more than a day. She came to me and begged me to run off with her, take her somewhere else, and make her my wife."

"You refused her, of course."

He nodded. "I did." He heaved a deep breath and let it out slowly. "She continued to resist her duty and finally concocted a vile plan."

Juliana wondered if she wanted to hear this. But she suspected he talked of it too little, which perhaps kept the wound from healing. And she felt privileged, in an odd way, to be the recipient of his confidence. "What was it?"

"She attempted to seduce me, hoping, I suppose, that my conscience would force me to marry her once I'd bedded her. When she was unable to do that, she...I do not know exactly what she did. But she got herself pregnant—not by me—and then told my family 'twas I had done it."

He shrugged. "What could I have in honor done then? I denied it, but she had carefully arranged for witnesses to her attempts at seduction, and some were cleverly set up. To all it appeared my guilt was certain. My brother, Edwin, was devastated, of course, and my family furious with me."

He sighed heavily. "I made all the apologies I could, and explained as much as I was able. Then Margaret died in childbed, and I could stay there no longer. Fortunately, I had friends in need of a strong arm in battle and assistance in maintaining the peace of their lands."

It wasn't until he turned to look at her that Juliana realized she'd stopped working on his hair and just held on tightly. Too tightly, no doubt, but the devastating guilt twisted her stomach into a knot.

His compassionate tone felt like another knife driven into her heart when he said, "My lady, be not so horrified on my behalf. 'Tis long past, now. I've tried to commit her to God's mercy. Christ does enjoin us to forgive those who have trespassed against as we wish forgiveness extended to ourselves." The tone changed to lightly ironic when he added, "I struggle with it."

Juliana released her hold on his hair as she tried to collect her wits. "That was a truly terrible thing she did to you, though. To betray you and her duty thus." Her breath stuck in her throat and her heart pounded too hard.

He put a gentle hand on her cheek. "My lady, I'm grateful for your compassion and concern on my behalf, but take it not too much to your heart. You have burdens enough already."

She winced. Her conscience did indeed carry too many burdens; how could she add to it the burden of betraying him again?

His fingers were warm on the skin of her face. Small pinwheels of excitement rushed into her where he touched, settling in her stomach. It was nearly unbearable, yet so pleasant and comforting at the same time, she couldn't bring herself to break the contact.

His breath caught as his hand moved against her cheek. His palm brushed the skin, and fingers threaded into her hair. His gaze caught hers from a distance of only inches away. He watched her with so much intensity in his blue eyes, she couldn't bear the scrutiny and looked down. His chest was magnificent, the skin sleek, the muscles shapely, and his flat brown nipples just peering out of the mat of fine, blond hair.

It wasn't a good idea, but she couldn't resist putting a hand out to feel it, stroking down the hard flesh, feeling its warmth, the ridges, the way it rippled as he tensed.

They shouldn't be doing this. She was betraying him all over again. She shouldn't be enjoying the feel of flesh against flesh so much. The closeness not only set her senses ablaze, making the warmth sing in her blood, but it found all the empty, lonely, emotionally starved crevices in her heart and began to fill them in. Why could Groswick not have been more like this man, with his sense of honor and compassion and kindness?

A strangled sob came from her throat.

"Hush," he said, very gently, and leaned forward to kiss her.

The pressure of his mouth against hers revealed an entire new world of sensation. She'd never realized lips could feel so much. The excitement of it stirred her blood, made it ripple and skip in her veins. It was heat pouring into her.

When he opened his mouth and probed delicately with his tongue, the jolt made her tighten all the way down to her toes. It was like nothing she'd ever known before. He was like no other man she'd met. But they shouldn't be doing this. She shouldn't be allowing it.

She opened her mouth to protest, but no sound came out. Instead he recognized the invitation she might or might not have meant to issue and inserted his tongue through the opening.

Her knees went weak and she clutched at his shoulders for support. Fire spread through her, settling in her middle, then sinking lower. She leaned against him, wanting nothing more than to be closer, even closer to him. His tongue swiped over her teeth and stroked hers. Her deep groan didn't make it out. She wanted to draw him as deeply into herself as it was possible to be.

As if her thoughts had communicated themselves to him, he put an arm around her shoulders and his other hand behind her head to draw her closer. His tongue withdrew for a moment and he nipped at her lips, then licked across them to soothe the exciting little ache.

Strange noises came from her, something between a sob and a pant. He kissed across her cheek to her ear, then down along her throat. Wherever his lips touched, the skin seemed to come alive, to tingle with the thrill of it.

She put both hands flat against his chest and felt the strong, rapid thudding of his heart. Her body shook with craving. She wanted this more than anything she could remember. But it was wrong. "My lord," she said, the words half plea and half protest.

He drew a deep breath and released her. "My lady, forgive me." He reached for her hand and stroked his palm over the back of it. "I should not have done that. But you're so very lovely and desirable, and I've been long without a lady's companionship. I do beg your forgiveness."

"Nay, my lord, there is naught to forgive. The guilt is as much mine. I, too, have been long without a man's companionship, and in truth…"

"In truth?"

Did she have the right to say anything of Groswick's shortcomings? "In truth, this is unlike anything I've ever known. Lord Groswick was not a man of great...patience."

He studied her. "This is a question I may have no right to ask, save that after...what just occurred between us, I would like to know. Have you ever known a woman's complete fulfillment, Lady Juliana?"

She shook her head. "I'm not sure what a woman's complete fulfillment might be. I don't believe I've ever experienced it."

He grinned. "If you don't know, you haven't." The smile faded, though he continued to study her. The soap was starting to dry in his hair. "Juliana, you believe your husband is dead, do you not?"

She drew a deep breath and steadied herself. "Aye, I do."

"Do you grieve for him?"

This was dangerous, but she owed it to him to be as honest as she could. "Not much, my lord. I regret that it appears he is dead, and any possibility of change is lost to him. I would not wish that. But... He was not... We were not..." She didn't know how to say it without sounding as though she complained or blamed Groswick for what might be her failures.

"You did not have much sympathy for each other?"

"Aye. What he needed, I was unable to give him."

"What was that?"

She smiled, though it felt hollow and empty. "If I'd known, perhaps I could have found it for him."

"True. And what of your needs?"

"What of them, my lord?"

"He did not try to satisfy your needs?

She shrugged. "It was not in his nature to understand such things."

"Or to try to understand."

"Groswick was what he was."

His smile held a level of understanding that made her heart clench. Before the tears could start, she said, "Perhaps you'd best sit down again, Sir Thomas, and allow me to rinse the soap out of your hair. You do not wish it to dry in."

"I'm sure I don't," he answered, while sinking back into the water. He was quiet for some moments while she carefully rinsed his hair. When she was done, he startled her by asking, "Has anyone ever assisted you in your bath, Lady Juliana?"

"Nay, my lord. 'Tis a task I can do for myself."

"Ah, but 'tis much more satisfying to have assistance. Tomorrow night, arrange for the servants to bring the bath here again. But this time, I'll wash you."

Chapter Five

After taking some food the next morning, Thomas ventured outside the keep to talk to some of the workers in the shops and work spaces around the bailey. Ralf had wandered into the great hall as he was finishing his meal. Rather than be left behind, the squire grabbed an apple and came with him.

"Talked to a couple of the maids last night," Ralf reported.

Thomas raised an eyebrow at him. "Just talked?"

Ralf shrugged and grinned in a way that suggested more than talk might have happened. The boy did have a way with ladies.

"Tried to get them to discuss Lord Groswick and how he left. They were wary of talking of him, but I kept trying and eventually they let loose a bit. 'Tis peculiar, though. They said little, and when one started to say something more, one of the others broke in with something inconsequential and stopped her."

The boy took a bite and chewed thoughtfully for a moment. "I could almost swear one of them signaled the other to be quiet then, too. As though there were something they shouldn't be saying."

"I should say 'tis good to know they can practice some discretion."

"Aye, I suppose so, but 'tis very strange, my lord."

"How so?"

Ralf shrugged again and spit out a seed. "In most keeps, there is endless gossip about the nobles of the place. Every detail of their lives is tossed about and discussed at great length. Here... Everyone will speak of the lady and how sweet she is, and how she cares for all, and how well she manages the keep and the demesne. None will talk of Lord Groswick. Should they start, they'll either catch themselves and stop or someone else will catch them and divert the conversation. Three times yesterday it occurred."

Thomas stopped and faced Ralf. "Aye, that is odd. Did you get any feeling of why they wouldn't speak of him?"

"Nay, my lord. It did seem that they feared him, perhaps. But why should that be when he's not here, and has not been for nigh onto a year?"

"Why indeed?" Thomas asked the question of himself as much as of Ralf. "I can think of any number of reasons, but cannot say I have any reason to favor one over another."

Ralf nodded. "Another thing. As I was entering the kitchen yesterday, I overheard part of a conversation. I heard your name mentioned, so I stopped where they couldn't see me and listened." He stopped and a wash of color lit his cheeks. "I know 'tis not very honorable to eavesdrop on others' conversations, but in this instance, things were being said that would have made it embarrassing both for myself and for those speaking should I have made my presence known at that moment."

Sir Thomas just raised an eyebrow at him.

"'Twas some of your more interesting qualities they discussed, my lord. It appears some here believe the Lady

Juliana favors you. One person commented that the lady looked at you in a certain way." The boy shrugged. "I know not what they meant by that, but they went on to talk of what features of yours interested her."

Thomas laughed at the boy's expression. "Please spare me the details. My pride needs no inflating." Nor did he need reminding of just how much the lady appealed to *him*. He couldn't easily forget that kiss last night and the way it set his body aflame, raging with need and desire.

"Aye. Or rather, nay!" Ralf colored again.

"Do not worry about it," Thomas ordered. "What else was said?"

They had to wait a moment, however, while a group of laughing, shouting children nearly bowled them over as they ran toward a side door of the keep, bearing baskets of fruit. Ralf waited until they'd passed before he continued.

"The rest of it concerned how Lady Juliana had suffered much and was deserving of some happiness. Some said they hoped she would find it with you. Others objected, saying you were a danger to her and she'd be well rid of you. But then someone reminded them that Lady Juliana had ordered you were not to be harmed. Nor any of those with you."

"Now that is interesting," Thomas remarked.

"Aye. Unfortunately at that moment I heard someone approaching, so I thought I'd best make some noise to warn them I approached, and go in."

Thomas nodded. "I'm pleased to hear she does not want us harmed." He wasn't sure how much of the irony Ralf understood.

But at that moment, they stood before the door of the smith's workshop. A ringing, clanking sound from within suggested the smith was at work. As soon as they entered, the noise grew to ear-numbing proportions and heat assailed them from the red hot coals of three separate fires.

A tall, almost gangly man looked up from the anvil where he hammered a piece of glowing iron into what looked like it would end up being a hinge of some kind. Two boys, one no more than eight or nine, the other closer to Ralf's sixteen, scurried around, bringing wood and water and fetching tools for the smith.

"Welcome, gentlemen," the smith said. He had a deep, rough voice, but his tone was pleasant. "Sir Thomas, is it not? And your squire. Do come in. I'm Robert the Smith. What can I do for you?" His smile seemed open and hearty enough, but wary caution lurked in his dark eyes.

"I have a pair of rings coming loose in my hauberk," Thomas told him. "I wondered if you'd have the time to repair it while I'm here?"

The man watched him steadily. "How long do you plan to be with us, Sir Thomas?"

"Until the mission the king gave me is concluded. I plan for a sennight or somewhat more."

Robert nodded. "Bring it to me anon and I can repair it for you."

"You're not over-busy right now then?"

"I stay moderately busy. But I have time to do work for honored guests."

"And I'm grateful for it. I suppose 'tis quieter with Lord Groswick away."

The man's eyes narrowed and his expression grew even warier. "There is always work to be done. If it's not swords, there are hinges, buckles, ploughshares, hoes, a world of other tools to be forged."

"No doubt. I understand Lady Juliana runs the household very efficiently, so you would be kept busy keeping things in order."

The smith nodded. "'Tis so, my lord."

"It must have been an added burden to you when Lord Groswick was preparing to leave. No doubt there were many things to supply or repair."

"Just so, my lord."

Thomas turned to Ralf and asked him to fetch the hauberk and show Robert where it needed repair. Ralf nodded and left.

"This year must have been very difficult for Lady Juliana. With Lord Groswick gone, she's had to bear a great deal of responsibility."

"Aye, but she's a strong lady for all her youth. And Lady Ardsley has been a help, though the last few months she's weakened. I fear she will not last much longer. 'Twill be a sad day for the lady when her mother passes."

Thomas recognized the diversion, but went with it, hoping he could glean some useful information from it.

"She'll truly be alone then. Has she no other family to help her?"

"None that I know of, my lord."

"That is sad. And she's so very young still. Think you she'll marry again?"

The man watched him for a moment before he shrugged. "We do not know with any certainty that Lord Groswick no longer lives. As to her plans in either case, I cannot say. 'Tis not for me to speculate."

Thomas commended the man for his discretion and was annoyed by it at the same time. He continued to question the smith a while longer, but was able to shake loose no further information. He bid the man good-day and went to look for another source.

The next several buildings were barns and storehouses. He found one groom in the barn, but the boy was slow-witted and no help at all.

Two doors down he found the cooper and his three apprentices. All looked up from a large cask they were putting together when he entered.

"Sir Thomas!" The master cooper was a large, paunchy, mostly bald man with a booming voice. "Welcome to our workshop. I'm Stephen the Cooper, this is Edward, Alwyn, and Gwynn." He pointed to each of the three boys who held gently curved staves in place while he bound them with some kind of wire. "How can we serve you, my lord?"

He had no personal task for this group, so he went directly to his purpose. "As you likely know, the king sent me to inquire as to the fate of Lord Groswick. It grieves His Majesty to know that one of his barons appears to have disappeared from the earth."

"Ah, no doubt," the cooper said, though his tone belied the words, suggesting some reservations on the question of whether the king was concerned about this particular baron. "I doubt there's much I can tell you others haven't, my lord. Lord Groswick left late last year, saying he was going to join the Prince on the Continent. So far as I know, none here has seen or heard from him since."

Thomas questioned him for some time, but as predicted, he heard nothing he hadn't known before. The man was garrulous, however, and Thomas spent over an hour with him, learning more than he'd ever wanted to know of the cooper's art, the weather, the crops, the other residents of the keep, and the history of the building itself. None of it offered any help to him in his mission, however.

He returned to the keep in mid-afternoon, intending to question some of the household servants himself. He was beginning to feel the need to learn more of Lord Groswick, his manner and habits. Perhaps in that he could begin to get some sense of why the man had disappeared, or what might have become of him.

However, as he passed Lady Juliana's workroom, he looked in and realized the lady was there, sitting at the desk, going over what appeared to be a ledger book. She didn't hear him, so he stopped in the doorway to admire her. A few dark curls had escaped from the coronet under her veil and spilled down her temples and around her ears. As she read over the lines on the paper, she twirled one of those strands around her finger. He doubted she realized she was doing it.

She looked incredibly young, sitting in the chair her late husband would have filled better, doing work that should have been his. Yet she was calm and at rest, clearly competent for this task. The line of her throat described a lovely curve and the flesh there looked soft and ripe. He wanted to go and kiss it until she moaned and begged for him. He wanted to lift the burden of too much responsibility from her shoulders.

Juliana looked up suddenly and met his eyes. A welcoming smile spread across her face as she called his name. "Sir Thomas! Come in, please. I trust you had a restful night."

His heart squeezed at the way his presence brightened her expression. He took the chair opposite her. "Quite. Yourself?"

"I did, my lord."

"I'm glad, as I had the advantage of a glorious bath and an excellent head rub. Tonight we shall reverse that. You will be sure to order the bath, my lady."

"My lord, this—"

He stopped her by putting his finger across her lips. "Nay, my lady. I'll do nothing you object to, but I will return some of the comfort you gave me."

"But—"

He cupped her cheek with his hand. "Juliana, do you truly believe Lord Groswick yet lives?"

She blinked at him, trying to hold back tears that made her eyes shine. "Nay, my lord. He does not."

"So I'm coming to believe. He is either dead, most likely on some distant battlefield or victim of brigands somewhere between here and there, or he is hiding and wants not to be found. I can think of no reason why he should do so, nor has anyone here offered any reasons. Can you think of any?

She sighed. "Nay. He had enemies, of a certainty, but were he to decide to hide out anywhere, 'twould be right here, in this keep, where he grew up, and where he knew he owned all in sight. That was greatly important to him. So, as he is not here now, I do not believe it likely he ever will return." Her fingers threaded together into a tight knot and her breath caught on a sob with the last word.

"Therefore you do not dishonor your marriage vows if you find you feel some desire for myself."

She gave him a wry and still slightly teary grin. "You assume much, my lord, that you should think I feel something for you."

"I do not assume, Juliana. I look in your face, in your eyes, and I see the passion that lurks, that rouses when you look at me. I do not think Lord Groswick ever roused that passion in you."

She sucked in a sharp breath. Dismay flashed across her face then was forcibly repressed. "Nay, my lord," she said, softly, almost a whisper. "He did not."

He leaned forward, running a gentle finger across her soft, full lips, watching the way her expression changed, her eyes darkening, her mouth parting. "There is something building between us. Your have no husband now, lady. You're free to explore what comes to us." Of course, he still had to prove that, but he would. He would.

She closed her eyes, almost wincing in what appeared to be pain. "Nay, my lord. I'm not free. I cannot be. There is more…there are things you do not know. Cannot know. I'll never be free. Not for you. Nor for any man."

"You still grieve?"

"Nay. Or rather, aye. I grieve. I grieve for many things."

"'Tis too early to look to the future for you?" He was startled by the realization, but it wasn't too early for him. In just a day or so, this lovely lady had come to represent all he wanted in life. She was warmth and love and home.

She leaned back. For a moment her eyes lost focus as though she stared into that future. Her expression went bleak. When she looked at him again, a yearning so deep and so intense it tugged at his heart flared in her eyes. It didn't last. She turned to stare out the window. "There are yet too many things that remain to be settled before I can look to the future, my lord."

"Then will you, at least, take some comfort in the present?" Instead of giving her time to answer, he dipped his head and pressed his lips to hers. She tasted sweet, flower sweet, honey sweet, like a perfectly ripe fruit. At first she remained unmoving, perhaps startled by the forwardness of his act. But after a minute she relaxed and her mouth softened.

He moved closer to her and drew her to her feet without releasing her mouth. His arms circled around her, pulling her body against him, chest to chest. She fit perfectly in his arms, her head resting on his shoulder. Heat poured through him. His cock rose to attention.

Though he knew her a strong and competent young woman, and admired her for it, she seemed remarkably small, delicate, almost fragile in his arms. The warmth of her body lit fires in his, while the feel of her skin turned his desire for her into a raging need. He'd known other women, had bedded a few, admired his friends' wives, but he'd never wanted anyone with this possessive ferocity. It surprised him to feel that way about a woman he'd known such a short time. But something in his soul seemed to recognize it had met its mate in her. In deep, important ways, Juliana resembled those other women he'd admired and even, though he rebuked himself for it, coveted.

He let his lips trail along the line of the scar on her temple. She'd never acquire any further scars if he could do anything to stop it. He caught the thought and followed where it led. It was too soon, and perhaps he went too far too quickly, but Juliana would some day be his. He hoped the day might not be far off, though there was still the complication of her missing and surely dead husband to be unraveled. But it would be, and then he would offer for her. The king had promised a substantial reward for fulfilling his mission, enough to keep them. His majesty would surely approve Thomas' request for the lady's hand.

The small sounds she made as he kissed and teased her sank into his soul like music. He could scarce bear to wait for the time he'd hear those little moans and more.

His hands rubbed her back and sides, stroking her graceful curves, feeling the line of her hip, waist, and up to her chest. He pushed her cap off and undid the braids that held her hair up, letting it fall in a glorious, silken mass over her shoulders and down her back.

She relaxed into his embrace, holding onto him and squeezing herself toward him. He splayed his hands on her sides, so that his fingers were just touching the undersides of her breasts. Her sharp breath hit him right in the chest like an arrow to the heart.

A sound outside the door, just down the hall, reminded them they were not alone or particularly private. Juliana jumped back, her breath harsh and panting. A servant went on past the entrance, intent on his own errand. She dropped back into her chair and began to rebraid her hair, though she continued to watch him.

Thomas touched her face, traced the line of the scar on her temple with a finger. "How did this happen?"

For a moment she remained quiet. "An accident with a piece of broken pottery a few years ago."

"You were fortunate it came no closer to your eye."

She sighed and nodded. "Very fortunate."

"Juliana—"

The lady looked up at him, eyes wide and still soft with passion and… "Sir Thomas." Her smile was gentle and sweet. "I am comforted. And for that I do thank you a great deal."

He felt a somewhat more wry grin twist his own mouth. "You'll arrange for the bath tonight."

After a moment, she nodded and gave him a smile. Then she turned to get back in her chair. But as he was leaving she stopped him. "Sir Thomas? Might I ask a favor of you?"

"Whatever you will, my lady."

For a moment her eyes widened and her gaze lost focus, but then she shook herself out of it. "I worry about our defenses here. We have no knights and few skilled men at arms. Would you review our guards and their deployment and tell me what we might do to improve? We have a few more young men eager to learn, but no one well qualified to train them. Samuel of Merimon is our captain and I believe him competent enough, but he has little imagination or patience.

Thomas nodded. "I'll do so. I have a few more of your household I'd like to question today. If you'll let your captain know about it, tomorrow I'll review your defenses with him."

Her smile held both relief and gratitude. He felt it more than adequate payment for whatever effort he put forth on her behalf.

* * * * *

Thomas found the bailiff, William Randolph, conferring with the steward. Randolph pointedly ignored him, continuing his conversation, despite the demands of rank and courtesy that would obligate him to acknowledge Sir Thomas at the very least.

When Thomas said, "Master Randolph, if I might have a word with you," the man gave him a concentrated glare that warned the interview would likely be less than pleasant.

"You want to ask me about Lord Groswick, my lord? I've heard you've been questioning others in the household." Randolph's tone told Thomas exactly how he felt about the activity.

Hoping to keep the unpleasantness to a minimum, Thomas reminded him, "I've been commissioned by the king himself to make inquiries. I regret that it causes disruption and perhaps some grief to the household here, but the king would know — if it's possible to learn — what became of Lord Groswick." He kept his irritation under control and his tone even.

Randolph gave him a jerky nod and said, "This way, my lord." He led the way to a small, quiet room a couple of doors down from the storeroom. "We can be private in here."

There were no chairs in the room, just one rough table, a few shelves bearing what looked like kitchen utensils, and rolls of fabric leaning against the wall. The window looked out onto the side of the bailey, toward the smith's shop he'd visited earlier. It also had a narrow ledge beneath it, which Thomas perched on.

"How long have you been bailiff here?" he asked Randolph.

The man looked surprised. Clearly that wasn't the question he'd expected. "Some ten years now. Since Milton Ashwood died."

"So you worked with Lord Groswick extensively."

"Aye."

Thomas waited a moment, but Randolph wasn't volunteering anything. "And you were here when he left."

"Aye."

"How long ago was that? Do you remember the exact day?"

The man drew a deep breath and shrugged. "Not the day itself. 'Twas in November, though early in the month. He wanted to set out before the weather turned."

"He was leaving it rather late at that, was he not?"

"He would wait until the harvest was done."

"Ah. He needed to be well-provisioned for the trip. How many men accompanied him? And were they keep men?"

"My memory is not entirely reliable, my lord, but as best I can remember, he went off with about three dozen men. Most were mercenaries, old friends, or those who owed debts he called on to support him. Only a very few belonged to the keep."

"Have you a list of their names?"

The man's hands clenched tight. "So far as I know, there is no list, my lord."

"Can you remember who they might be?"

"I can give you a few names." He rattled off a list that was just as unspecific as the one the cook had given him.

Thomas did note a few whose families he recognized and committed those to memory to inquire about later.

"Tell me about Lord Groswick," Thomas asked. "What manner of man was he? Was he an easy man to work with?"

Randolph's eyes narrowed and his lips pinched together for a moment. "He was no easy man, Lord Groswick."

Again Thomas waited, but Randolph declined to elaborate. "In what way?" he prompted.

Randolph looked around as though searching for a way to escape the room. "His temper was uncertain at the best of times. His manner…he was the lord. That was all. He felt no need to be kind or merciful, or even just. He regarded not the feelings or rights of others, including his household and those closest to him. When things were not to his liking, he would often react…quite violently."

"Violently? How so?"

The man's breathing had quickened. "He… He could be quite loud in his reproaches. And he injured a few people who did not please him."

"Injured. He struck them?"

"Aye, my lord."

"Then people here feared him?"

"Aye, my lord. That they did. Many would duck and hide when they saw him approach."

"Then I should suppose many were relieved when he left."

The man hesitated. "Aye, that they were."

"And all are happier with Lady Juliana running the keep?"

"Indeed. The lady is quite adept at it. She's much better at organizing affairs and keeping them running smoothly than my Lord Groswick was. And she has a way with people as well."

"What will happen when Lord Groswick returns?" Thomas asked him.

The man froze as he turned to look at something outside. His face paled and his eyes widened. He took two deep harsh breaths before he responded. "Do you think it likely he'll return, my lord? You said he never met the Prince and no one has heard from him."

"I think all here are hoping he will not. But you know the king will grant the lordship to someone else of his choosing once he's convinced Lord Groswick is dead."

"Aye, I know. Is that all, my lord?"

"Nay, are you this insolent when dealing with Lady Juliana?"

The man turned whiter, then a tide of red crept up under his skin. "Nay, my lord. I beg your pardon. I meant no offense. 'Tis just that I worry for Lady Juliana. I fear your inquiries can only cause her pain and make her situation worse. Please, my lord, if you have any compassion for her, leave here now and ask no more questions."

"And what would you suggest I tell the king?"

"Tell him Lord Groswick has disappeared and you have no idea where he has gone."

"Right now, that is, in fact, all I know to be true," Sir Thomas admitted.

Chapter Six

Juliana seemed more apprehensive than usual at dinner that evening. The smile she gave to those around her as she made her way to the table on the dais looked forced and faded too quickly. Her hand even shook a bit when she picked up her cup.

"My lady, are you nervous?" he asked.

She turned a surprised look on him. "Why do you think that, my lord?"

He nodded to the drops of red wine splashed on the white table cloth. "Your hand is less than steady."

She sighed and set the cup back down. A small drop of red wine clung to a corner of her mouth. He wanted to kiss it off, but contented himself with wiping his finger across it, collecting the moisture. As she watched, eyes wide and yearning, he brought the finger to his mouth and licked the droplet of wine off it.

"I suppose I'm not quite… Aye, I'm somewhat tense."

"Is it the bath I promised you?" He spoke low so that only she could hear his words. He loved the way the rose pink blush colored her cheeks. "Juliana, if you truly don't wish it, I'll not force it on you. I'll never force anything on you you don't want. And if we go ahead, and I do anything you don't like, you've but to say the word and I'll stop. Do you trust me that far?"

She looked up at him and nodded. Her hesitance suggested the decision to trust was not an easy one for her.

What had Lord Groswick done to her to make her this way? Still, his heart expanded at that sign of confidence in him.

Dinner took too long. Far too long. Though he enjoyed the food, the wine, and the conversation, he wanted it over long before it was.

And then afterward, he had to wait for her to arrive. The tub was set up and servants hauled buckets of water to fill it as he got back to his quarters after the meal. He sent Ralf and Bertram off again. Ralf had the cheek to give him a crooked grin and a wink as he left, and ducked a feigned blow.

"Have a good evening, my lord," Ralf wished him as he left. "Do not swim too deep." It was a tease, but there was also a hint of warning there. Thomas didn't make the mistake of disregarding it completely.

"I'll swim no deeper than I may. I have no plans to drown here."

The boy nodded and left.

Juliana entered a few minutes later, unescorted. She looked around with guilty hesitance.

"We're private here," he said. "My men will not interrupt. Would you have me bar the door so none may enter, or would you feel more secure were I to leave it unbarred that you may run away from me more quickly?"

Her smile was small and nervous still. "Have many ladies felt the need to flee your presence, Sir Thomas?"

"Only a few. My sister once, when I pulled her hair and tormented her until she kicked me and then fled in fear of my wrath. A wh... A woman of ill repute who thought to rob me when I caught her in the act of going through my purse. By and large, though, the few ladies

I've allowed in my quarters have felt no need for a fast exit."

"I believe I'll trust to your word earlier." She licked her lips and swallowed hard. "Sir Thomas—"

He was at her side as fast as he could move and put a finger over her lips. "Nay. No objections. We both believe you have no husband, lady. If he be not dead, and I do believe it is so, he's most certainly dishonored your vows by remaining away so long. I cannot believe you'll ever see him again. You've been too long now carrying the burden of this place on yourself with none to comfort you."

"Save my mother."

"Save your mother. But while mothers can offer a great deal of comfort, there is a kind that can only flow between a man and a woman."

"But I've no right to—"

"Say no more," he ordered. "I will not take from you that which only your husband may by right have. But tonight I take all burdens on myself. For tonight you are completely in my hands and in my power. You'll forget all else and do only as I command, save that if there is anything you truly don't wish or can't abide, you have but to tell me and I'll stop. What say you, lady? Will you give all responsibility into my keeping for this night?"

She frowned. "I do not understand."

He put his hands on her shoulders. "You lay responsibility for all that happens tonight on me, by agreeing now that you will do whatever I order you to do, save that it truly offends you. You put yourself completely in my control. I give my word I'll not have a husband's way with you, but will only do what will comfort and please you. We'll call it your penance that your hospitality was initially so cold when I arrived. You kept me waiting out in the rain far longer than you should have. In recompense, for this night, you will serve me exactly as I demand."

A slow, almost shy, smile spread over her face as she understood what he wanted. "Ah, I see, my lord. Our hospitality was lacking that day, and I suppose I do owe you some penance for that. If this is how you would have it, then I offer it to you." Her expression turned suddenly arch. "But, my lord, should I fail to obey a command?"

"I'll have to punish you, of course. A loving punishment."

Her eyes widened and a sparkle burst to life in them. She opened her mouth, but couldn't quite bring herself to ask the next question. It didn't matter. She'd already accepted the invitation and was intrigued by the game, though that didn't drive away all her apprehension.

"We're wasting the hot water," he said. "I'll play your maid and help you disrobe."

He fumbled only a bit with the laces and tapes of her garments, and that more because the sight of her gradually revealed, lovely body made him shake with need and desire for her rather than any innate clumsiness. Though Juliana was quiet while he undid and removed her overgown, her harsh breathing and the fine trembling of her body revealed her nervous excitement. When he loosened the tape at the back of her shift, she sucked in a sharp breath and said, "Sir Thomas —"

"Nay, lady," he cut her off. "Do you forget already you've given yourself to my use in penance?" She didn't resist when he pushed the loose shift off her shoulders and guided it down her arms until it fell to the floor by its own weight. Without thinking, she crossed her arms over her front, attempting to hide her lovely breasts and the secrets hidden at the cleft of her legs.

He didn't object. The struggle to control the raging desire of his engorged cock took much of his effort. She was so beautiful, so gloriously, gracefully curved, yet sleek and tight. He wanted to touch her so much that sweat beaded on his temple as he fought the urge.

"Into the tub with you," he said. His voice didn't sound quite steady.

She drew a deep, long breath and walked to the tub. He helped her in and turned away for a moment to find the remnants of his self-control. Once he thought he could keep himself in line, he picked up a washcloth and soap, and sat on the stool next to the tub, just as she had done the previous evening.

He wasn't at all surprised to see she'd slid down the side far enough to submerge all but the top third of her breasts. Even so he fought to drag his gaze from the most exquisite and delectable span of flesh he'd ever seen. He couldn't imagine any man going off and leaving her. When she was his, it would take a team of a dozen horses or more to drag him away from her side.

Thomas began to rub the soapy washcloth over her shoulders and down her arms. If she got any more tense, she'd break. Her muscles were as tight and hard as rocks. Remembering how good it had felt when she'd rubbed the soap into his hair yesterday, he set down the washcloth and moved the stool around behind her.

"Duck your head," he asked. "We'll start with your hair."

She did as he ordered with no objection. Rubbing the soap into her long hair did slowly relax her and had the advantage of soothing his raging need somewhat as well. He liked the feel of burying his fingers in her hair, smoothing soap all along the length of the gently curling strands, and massaging her scalp, far more than he expected. That Juliana calmed down under the care was a pleasant bonus. His heart swelled with the knowledge he could help her.

She grew so quiet and relaxed he had to ask, "Are you asleep, my lady?"

"Nay." Her voice was lower and husky, but not, he thought, with sleep. "It does feel wondrously pleasant, however."

"Good. That was my purpose. But the water begins to cool. Rinse the soap from your hair." She did so. It gave him another thrill to have her obeying his orders and trusting to his care.

"Now lean forward. You'll like this as well." He rubbed more soap on a cloth and began to scrub her back. She sucked in a breath, then let it out on a long, gusty sigh. Her shoulders flexed and twitched as he ran the cloth up and down her spine, going down to just above her waist.

"That does feel marvelous, my lord."

He continued to rub a few minutes longer, until a shiver warned him the water was cooling fast.

"Out now, lady," he said, tossing aside the cloth and finding the larger towel. She looked up at him with wide eyes.

"Stand," he said, making the word hard enough to be an order.

She nodded, sighed again, and pushed herself upright.

"You need not be ashamed of your body," he told her. "It's a wondrous and beautiful body."

"Save for the scars."

"Ennobled by the scars. I have a few myself. They tell the world you have lived and experienced both the joy and the pain." He ran a gentle finger over the scar on her temple. "Only I think you've had little of the joy and much of the pain."

"I've known joy, my lord."

"Every day?" he asked. "With Lord Groswick?"

She bit her lip before she shook her head. "Nay."

"Did you ever know any pleasure at all at his hands?"

"Nay."

Thomas couldn't decide whether to be furious with Groswick for treating his wife so coldly or grateful that it had been left to him to show her about the pleasures her body could afford her. "Then I have much to teach you." He helped her out of the tub and into her robe, then wrapped the towel around her wet hair. After he toweled her hair until it was half-dry, he laid her back on his bed.

She stared up at him, her green eyes wide. "Does it please you to teach me, my lord?"

"It does."

"'Tis a strange sort of penance," she admitted, "but I will not refuse it."

"Well that you don't."

Her smile was sweet and just a bit calculating. "I do not promise to be so accommodating all the time."

"And I would not expect it. It would be far too dull in any case. But for now—" He leaned over, and loosed the tie that held the robe together in front, then pushed the sides apart.

She gasped and tried to cover her breasts with her hands.

"Nay, lady." He gently lifted her hands and moved them away. "You're beautiful. You've no need to hide from me. And as you're under my command, you may not refuse or resist." Her breasts weren't large, but their shape was graceful and the rosy pink tips puckered delightfully. Such loveliness demanded a man's devotion; Thomas paid them reverence.

His cock throbbed at the sight. Unable to resist, he put out a hand and touched the tip of her left breast with just the end of his finger. She jerked in surprise, but also let out a gasp of pleasure. He ran his hands down her throat and chest, brushing over the breast, then repeated it on the other side. Her expression changed from surprise to delighted wonder.

He continued touching her breasts, sometimes stroking up and down, sometimes circling the nipples with his fingers. Her fine skin was soft as goose down. The plush mounds made perfect handfuls when he cupped them in his palms.

Juliana's breath caught several times as he toyed with her nipples, and her face tightened at the pleasurable tension his touches roused. She sighed, "My lord," when he squeezed the tip carefully, not too hard. He played with her for a while, drinking in her sighs and gasps, until his back protested about his leaning over at an awkward angle for too long.

He straightened up and said, "Roll over."

She gave him a wicked grin and shook her head in refusal.

So she wanted to play the game? He couldn't let her see how much that gratified him. "My lady," he said instead. "One last chance. Roll over. If I have to roll you over myself, your bottom will pay the price of your disobedience."

A flash of panic shot across her face, but when she glanced at him, whatever she saw seemed to reassure her. She just shook her head again and tried to look both stubborn and solemn.

It convinced him. He climbed onto the bed with her, shucking his tunic and loosening the laces of his shirt as he went. Kneeling beside her, he quickly flipped her over onto her belly and tugged the robe off her completely. It went to the floor also. He stopped, frozen for a moment by the sight of her completely nude body. She was long and quite lean, but her round derriere flared nicely. The smooth expanse of her back showed another scar up near her shoulder, but that did nothing to mar the splendor of her shape. Her damply curling hair spilled partly over it, making a pleasing contrast between the dark locks and the pale skin. Her bottom had the same smooth, white flesh. It would look even sweeter with the pink flush he was about to induce.

Still he couldn't resist running a hand over the rounded globes and watching her twitch in pleasurable but nervous anticipation.

"Now, my lady, a lesson in obedience for you." He raised his hand and smacked it down smartly but not very hard on her left bottom cheek. It gave under the force and sprang back. The skin whitened for a moment under the impact, then flushed pink. Juliana gasped but didn't move or protest. He slapped down on the other side to give it a matching rose blush. Six more spanks had her squirming. Another two drew a low moan.

"Tell me when you think you've learned to obey," he said. That would leave it up to her to decide when she'd had enough and give her a way to let him know.

It surprised him when it took almost two dozen more spanks before she finally sobbed and said, "I believe I've learned the lesson, my lord." By then her derriere was growing quite rosy, shading into red in places, and in truth, his hand was getting sore as well. She was one strong-willed lady.

He rolled her onto her back, keeping his eyes resolutely away from the cleft between her legs where he longed to explore, and instead gathering her into his arms. Unshed tears glazed her eyes, making his stomach twist in dismay.

"Juliana, did I hurt you? 'Twas not my intention! I thought you understood, 'twas all a game. You could stop it whenever you wished."

"I know that, Thomas." A grin made the tears still washing her eyes sparkle. "I did not want it to end too soon. It hurt, a little, but not so much. And it was very…exciting as well. The hurt seemed to change as it sank in and became something else."

"Ah, that's as it should be. And, now, my lady, as you've submitted your will to me, I have one more thing to show you." He set her back down on the bedcovers and leaned down to kiss her. His cock was so swollen it hurt to move, but he forced himself to ignore it. He licked across her lips and invaded the hot, sweet depths of her mouth, until she reached up and dragged him down, forcing him to stretch out next to her with her legs and chest against his.

He allowed it for a few minutes, then backed away and slid down the bed. As he did so, he ran his tongue down her throat and along her chest until he reached a breast. Making gentle circles, he licked around the right one, moving higher until he finally reached the tip. She squealed loudly when he licked across the nipple. He repeated the sequence on the other breast, tonguing the peak until she all but sobbed. With a gentle suction, he drew the tip into his mouth. The taste of her was sweeter than molasses, the texture of her skin finer than the smoothest pudding.

When he moved to the other side, she threaded her fingers into his hair and held onto him. The pressure in his groin beat so ferociously it took every bit of his will not to let it loose on her. When he knew he could take no more, he backed away and slid off the bed.

Her eyes widened and she looked puzzled. He came back and kissed her temple gently, then handed her the robe. "Enough for tonight. This is a feast not a snack, so we'll take each course in its time."

"As you wish, my lord." Her tone sounded the regret she refused to put into the words.

"'Tis better this way. Trust me."

"Aye," she agreed. "Then we'll meet again tomorrow night?"

"Save you do not wish it."

She laughed. "Oh, I'll wish it, Thomas. I wish it now more than I can say. But... Tomorrow night, it should be your turn to submit to me."

He turned to her, stunned at first, then feeling a laugh rise inside as it sank in. She wanted to play this game as much as he did. His joy in it struck so deep he almost spent on the spot. Fortunately he managed to contain it long enough to help her back into her robe and escort her down the hall to her solar.

His men weren't in sight, thank heavens, as he raced back to his chamber after kissing her one last time at her door. He got inside, bolted the door and settled back onto the bed, freeing himself of his clothing as he crossed the room. The bed groaned as he fell across it, a hand already pumping at his raging cock.

With the memory of Juliana's glorious, bare body fresh in his mind, the sweet taste and texture of her still pleasant on his tongue, her soft moans and squeals ringing in his ears, he wanted to make it last. But he couldn't take it slow. The force of his need refused to be contained. The pleasure rolled over and through him like a tidal wave, sweeping all his will and need before it. Three strokes of his hand up and down his cock and it spurted seed onto his hand and chest.

The relief was as enormous and welcome as the need had been hot and raging. He rested, spread across the bed, until he had his breathing back under control and he thought he could walk again. He felt a little guilty and a little foolish, but he could no more have stopped it than he could hold back the wind.

After a while, he got up and rang for the servants to clean up. How long a mourning period would be demanded, he wondered, once he delivered his report concerning the likely demise of Lord Groswick? How long before he could wed Juliana and make her his own in every possible way?

Chapter Seven

Juliana got through most of the morning without anyone noticing, or at least commenting on, how distracted she was. She dealt calmly with a dispute between a pair of crofters, a complaint by one of the dairymaids, a crisis in the kitchens over tallow for candles, and the discovery that mice had gotten into the linen closet.

No one reacted oddly to her or treated her any differently, so they likely didn't see the profound change within her, or the conflict tearing her apart.

Whether he knew it or not, Sir Thomas was laying siege to her heart, and she feared he wouldn't have to fight very hard to win command of it. She didn't know what to do about that. It felt both wonderful and agonizing at the same time.

Aside from her silly days back when she was eleven or twelve and had a crush on her stepfather's squire, no man had ever captured her interest this way.

She had long yearned for someone to love her in the way she'd heard of in stories told by minstrels and bards. Like most young girls, she'd adored listening to the tales of brave, handsome knights performing valiant deeds and rescuing lovely maidens who won their hearts. She'd quickly grown out of believing in such tales, but a secret yearning for it had lingered far back in her mind, even as she'd come to realize the only one who would rescue her from anything was herself.

Sir Thomas came dangerously close to being her fantasy knight, with his handsome looks and noble carriage. His kind heart and sense of humor completed the picture of a valiant and noble knight. He deserved better than the heartbreak she would bring him.

She was no beautiful, innocent maiden. Perhaps once she had been. But now she had ugly scars marring her face, thanks to the man who should have been her lord and protector. Worse, she had ugly stains on her soul as well.

She should stop whatever bloomed between herself and Sir Thomas before it turned to hate, as it would when he learned the truth. Was there any way out of this? Any way that wouldn't cause him heartbreak and pain?

"You were looking for me, my lady?"

The voice interrupted her uncomfortable musings. Juliana looked toward the door. "Peter, aye, I need to speak with you."

Among the servants and freemen, especially the female ones, Peter Randolph, the bailiff's son, displayed the cocky swagger of a barely restrained peacock. In her presence, though, he acted more subdued.

"The night he arrived here, someone fired a crossbow at Sir Thomas. I know you train with some of the other young men in using the crossbow, so you likely know who it was. I don't ask you to tell me, but I do ask that you make all aware I will not have Sir Thomas or any of his men injured or worse. Another such attempt will force me to take stronger action."

She studied the young man's face. His expression had slipped into a combination of fear and resentment.

"Will you tell all and be sure they understand how much I mean it?"

Peter nodded jerkily. "But, my lady... He is a danger to you. He'll learn what happened and report it to the king."

"Perhaps he'll learn the truth, and he'd likely report it to the king if he does. But if that happens, I'll face it. I'll not have anyone hurt or killed to prevent it happening."

"My lady, it's being told about that you shared his bed."

Her blood fired with a combination of embarrassment and anger. Her voice was harsh when she answered. "Should I have done so or not, 'tis no concern of yours."

"Aye, my lady, 'tis true. I beg your pardon." He made an awkward attempt at a bow. "We fear for you, my lady. No one here would have anything happen to you."

"I know that. But some things cannot be prevented. And some should not. Many things remain to be settled yet, and I know not how all of them will finish. I do know this, however. If Sir Thomas or his men are harmed, my conscience will never again know any rest at all. It will destroy me. And I will, I assure you, learn who did the deed and see them punished severely." She drew a breath and looked at the young man. "Let that be known to all."

He nodded, but there was still a mulishness about his expression that made her fear—for Sir Thomas, for herself, and for him as well.

"Aye, my lady. If I may be excused?" The boy bowed and made his exit.

Juliana got up and paced across the room a few times. A series of thunking sounds outside drew her to the window to watch the men-at-arms practicing in an enclosed court at the far end of the bailey. The noise she'd heard was the sound of arrows hitting wooden targets. An admirable number of them protruded from the wood, as only a dozen or so men practiced.

Closer to her window, another group watched as Sir Thomas demonstrated some technique of sword use. Given that he seemed to move in a fairly normal side to side manner, she couldn't guess what he showed them. The men, however, paid close attention, and several mimicked his motions with the blank wood swords they used for practice.

Then he showed them something involving a lunge. The sun glittered off his hair, turning it a bright gold color. He moved nimbly, with an agile grace surprising in a man who was taller than all but one of those gathered around him. The others attempted to mimic his action, and Sir Thomas moved among them, offering a word here, changing the angle of an arm there. Occasionally he exchanged a few words with one. The positions of their bodies told her the conversations were friendly and the men showed him considerable respect as well as good humor.

He would be the perfect lord for this keep—a man others admired and respected. An honorable, noble man. One she felt sure would treat justly with all to the best of his ability. And as he was an intelligent and very determined man, his ability should be considerable.

Perhaps they could continue to keep him in the dark about Lord Groswick's fate. Let him report to the king that Groswick remained missing and was likely dead on some foreign shore. Would the king make him baron of this estate as reward for his service? Give him her hand in marriage? If she made it clear she wished it, was it not likely?

She rested her head against the side of the window as she watched Sir Thomas walk among her men-at-arms, now showing them something involving a staff. These were good people who served them here. They'd suffered too much under Lord Groswick's heavy-handed rule and deserved better. They deserved a lord who would care for them, nurture them, protect them, and help them to a better life.

What did she deserve? She knew all too well the answer to that.

Juliana drew a long breath and tried not to sob as she let it out. She found a shawl and all but ran down to the chapel, which was empty at this time of day.

She sank down on a kneeling bench, praying and weeping at the same time. Her prayers were a muddled mix of pleas for forgiveness, for help for the people of Groswick, for peace for her mother, for Sir Thomas's safety, and guidance in what to do next.

Only one answer came to her, and it was of limited use. She could have a peaceful future here, if Sir Thomas would go away and not come back. It would be a lonely, empty time, made meaningful only by the necessity to do her duty for the land and people. If she wanted Sir Thomas in her future, however, she would have to be honest with him. He deserved that, even though it might indeed cost her his love. She couldn't live a lie with him, knowing he might—surely would!—someday learn the truth and have to make the agonizing choice of what to do about it.

She needed time, however. She couldn't tell him yet. Not until after her mother had passed to her rest. Of course even if she didn't tell him, he might not go away, and he might well find out what she'd done. What would he do then?

What she needed more than anything else, though, was strength. Strength to do what had to be done, and when it had to be done. Before she left the chapel, she said a pair of *Ave Marias* and *Pater Nosters* under her breath, begging for the courage and will she would need.

As if to mock her agony, on her way out of the chapel, a pair of servants came to tell her a company of entertainers had arrived and begged leave to perform for them that night. Her heart squeezed. How could she bear to watch the antics of tumblers and jugglers when she was torn so? Yet, it would bring pleasure to her people, and in that she found comfort and satisfaction.

"Bid them come in and be welcome," she told the servants as she went to consult with the weavers over needed linens.

Late in the afternoon, Sir Thomas found her in the kitchens, consulting with the cook over the use of a deer one of their hunters had brought in. She finished and went with him to her office to hear his report.

"Your defenses are not so bad as you fear, my lady," he said when they were private. "You have a decent fighting force, though their training is not as sharp as it might be. They're also somewhat young."

"A few years ago Groswick made an abortive raid on one of our neighbors to the north. It cost us many of our men."

"That was poorly done, unless he truly had reason to think he could conquer."

Juliana shrugged. "I know not. In truth I think he felt he needed to prove something. To his men, perhaps."

"Your captain is a competent leader and has a sensible approach to manning the fortifications. I made one or two suggestions to him that I expect he will employ. He's not as strong at training the men, though."

"I saw you demonstrating some moves to them earlier. 'Twould be well if you could stay for a time to train our troops. I believe you have the gift of it, Sir Thomas."

His expression went serious. The glow faded from his blue eyes. "Juliana, it would give me great pleasure to do so. But that decision is not mine. I have a mission to perform. When that is done, I hope to be able to return. To you and to your keep."

"It would please me."

Perhaps fortunately, the warning bell for dinner sounded at that moment.

Juliana could barely eat for the nerves tightening her stomach, yet at the same time she wished it would end all the quicker than it did. Further interaction with Sir Thomas of the sort they'd been having was dangerous—to her heart, her soul, and her spirit. But she'd more or less promised him this night, and she couldn't go back on her word.

The cooks provided a superb dinner of stewed venison so savory the aroma had her near to drooling before they began to eat. The taste lived up to the promise of the smell, with meat and vegetables tender enough to give easily when bitten, but not cooked mushy, and seasoned to perfection.

A day spent demonstrating fighting techniques and teaching her men to perform them put Sir Thomas in a high humor.

"Your cooks have done themselves proud yet again, my lady," he said after tasting the stew. "If the quality of the meals denotes the quality of the management of an estate, yours is among the best."

"Perhaps it does. Or perhaps it just signifies that we are fortunate to be blessed with such a talented head cook."

"A blessing indeed. I have a great, empty cavern in my stomach waiting to be blessed with this wonderful food."

"Is your stomach then a worthy chapel to contain such blessings?"

"I would not claim it so on my own. But with God's grace, aye, I believe it to be. Certainly it is eager to claim the blessing, so it will do whatever is necessary to be found worthy. Needs it your benediction as the lady of the keep?"

"I am not worthy to confer blessings of any sort, and only count myself fortunate for what little grace comes my way."

His gaze on her turned momentarily serious. "A great deal of grace resides in you, my lady, and flows from you at every word and every turn."

"Nay, my lord. 'Tis no false modesty when I say I can make little claim on any grace."

"You need make no claim, my lady. 'Tis already a part of you."

He would continue to say sweet words to her and flatter her throughout the meal despite her efforts to deflect him.

Once the meal had concluded, the troop of entertainers began to perform.

The group consisted of six men ranging in age from a youth no more than fifteen or sixteen to the leader, who was likely in his late thirties. They were good. So very good, in fact, that for a while even Juliana lost herself in amusement at their antics. The tumblers formed elaborate structures of human limbs by climbing all over each other and balancing in the most impossible positions. They bounced all around the hall, doing flips and cartwheels, handsprings and handstands. They rolled along benches, somersaulting the entire length of the plank, did handsprings over the tables and headstands on them.

They clowned as well, interacting with the people present. One lithe, handsome young man circled the room, kneeling or bowing before every woman in the place, making sheep's eyes at her, or presenting her a stiff cloth folded into various amazing shapes.

The audience laughed and clapped and had a marvelous time. Children screamed and cheered. Parents had to restrain rambunctious youngsters from attempting the same feats they'd just seen performed. Juliana's mother laughed until the tears streamed down her face and she struggled to get her breath again.

Seeing her gasp, Juliana would have called halt to the entertainment, but her mother would have none of it. "Nay, my dear," she insisted even as she strove to take a breath. "It has been far too long since we've had such merriment. In truth, I cannot remember ever hearing laughter such as this in this hall. Let it go on. I'm no worse than usual and I feel the joy lightening my soul."

Juliana nodded and acceded to her mother's wishes.

The tumblers ran to a corner of the room where they exchanged their multi-colored finery for another set. They brought back with them balls of various sizes and colors, sets of staves, stuffed cloth bags, and extra shoes and hats. Their juggling was a wonder to behold. Every one of them could sustain three balls in the air at once. They did it in harmony, with all of them tossing balls at exactly the same time and speed.

Then some of them changed the balls for long, round staves. They juggled those with even more aplomb, catching them and flipping them up end over end. Other jugglers added another ball or even two to the mix. A pair of them began tossing balls and staves back and forth while juggling. Shoes somehow became mixed in, with a juggler sometimes managing to pull one off his own foot and adding it into the batch without ever dropping anything. Then their hats also became part of the round robin juggling, flying back and forth.

By the end of the performance, the jugglers stood in a circle in the center of the hall, juggling from one to the next, passing each item around in a circle. Each performer took the item, juggled it a few times with the things he already had, then tossed an item onto the next one in the circle. Balls went around this way, but so did the staves, shoes, hats, drinking cups they'd borrowed from nearby tables, and even a couple of leftover bread trenchers. They kept it going for an amazingly long time before they all, at some unseen signal, tossed the items they had straight up in the air and caught each one.

Amidst laughter and applause, the performers bowed to the room, and then bowed to each other, over and over. It drew even more laughter from the crowd. Finally the one who appeared to be the leader of the group went down the line, turning each person to face the table where Juliana sat.

They bowed in unison.

"My lord and lady, 'tis a pleasure to perform before your household this night," the leader said. "I thank you for the gracious hospitality given and trust that we've provided some measure of amusement and entertainment for you this evening."

Juliana glanced toward Thomas. The amusement lit his face to a fine glow, making him even more stunningly handsome. He nodded to her and she stood, facing the group.

"Gentlemen, we are indeed highly entertained by your performance. I do believe, in fact, you've brought more joy and laughter to this hall than has been heard here in far too long. Avail yourselves of our hospitality for the night, and in the morning, I'll have for you a payment worthy of your performance."

The jugglers broke out in applause this time and they each did a handspring or cartwheel in reaction.

"Many thanks, indeed, my lady," the leader said. "And blessings be on this household."

Juliana bowed as well and then turned to leave the room. She heard Sir Thomas rise behind her. Others got up and began to clear off the tables, take them apart, and slide them aside to make room for those who would sleep in the hall.

She looked back to see if his men accompanied Sir Thomas. They didn't, and the grin he gave her made clear he would hold her to her word for the evening. Her stomach fluttered with a mix of excitement and doubt. She changed quickly into a fresh shift and a satin overrobe, taking off her cap and letting her hair hang loose. As she drew her comb through it to smooth it out, she realized how freeing her hair seemed to free her soul or spirit from the constraints of the day's duties.

Sir Thomas's door stood partly open, waiting for her. She pushed it closed behind her and dropped the bar into place.

He sat on the side of the bed. He'd already removed his tunic and boots and loosed the laces on his shirt.

"No bath tonight, I fear, my lord. I did not want to deny anyone the entertainment after dinner. There has been too little laughter within these walls."

"Of course. I would not have denied them either. Come here, Juliana."

She hesitated a moment, then walked toward him.

"I will deny you nothing, either," he said. "What would you have of me, my lady?"

She sucked in a sharp breath. There were many things she should demand of him. Go away. Leave us in peace. Stop searching for answers. Give me back my heart. Instead, she said, "Teach me how to please you, Sir Thomas."

He drew her toward him until she stood between his splayed legs. "You please me just by being who you are," he answered.

"When you know me better, you may not think so. But that was not what I intended."

"I know. Yet 'tis true, nonetheless." He pulled her into his arms, pushed the robe off, lifted the shift over her head, sat her on one of his muscular thighs, and kissed her until her head felt light and the heat ran up and down her body in a bubbly wave. She leaned into his chest, moaning with pleasure as he nibbled her lip and then stroked with his tongue.

"This pleases me a great deal." He shifted and the hard shaft of his cock rubbed against the side of her leg.

It pleased her as well. And when he put his big hands over her breasts and began stroking them, it pleased her even more. She sighed as the tingles spread from her breast, and gasped when he squeezed the tips just hard enough to make them burn.

His hand slid down from her breast over her belly toward the cleft between her legs. At the juncture, he paused and veered to the side, stroking along the top of her thigh. He rubbed down one and up the other, circling around again and again, moving a little more inward each time. His fingers left trails of tingling, sparking flesh as they passed.

A need to be closer to him, to touch him in the same way he touched her, rushed through her. Responding to it, Juliana reached under his shirt to put her hands on his chest. Warmth seeped into her palms where they rested on the strong muscles. She rubbed gently and felt a quiver ripple through him. What a wonder it was to realize she had that much power over this strong, powerful man. A need to cling to him, to hold him and not let him go, surged through her and squeezed her heart.

Then he nudged her thighs apart, his hand slipped into her cleft, and she stopped thinking for some time. She felt. Incredible surges of pleasure drove through her as he brushed along her quim. A moan flowed from her as his fingers invaded, separated, explored, stroked the sensitive, delicate petals of flesh. He found an even more lusciously sensitive spot, and the jolt made her body stiffen.

"What...What are you doing to me?"

"Showing you how a lady feels pleasure."

"I...I think I mentioned before you do well in training people."

"Ah, but I've just begun with you, Juliana. There is much more to learn."

He shifted and moved her onto the bed, laying her along it. He stroked over her breasts and belly again, making her sigh with wonder and joy. Need roused and settled, heavy and pulsing, low in her belly, squeezing her womb.

When he leaned over and pressed his lips against a nipple, tonguing it gently, she squealed with delight. Ribbons of pleasure threaded through her veins.

"Thomas," she said on a sigh. "How many more delights can you wring forth from my body? I never knew."

He released her nipple long enough to say, "Your husband was exceedingly remiss in his duties, then. 'Tis a husband's right and privilege to teach his wife such pleasures."

"But you are not—"

He stopped the words with a kiss. "Nay, I am not. With God's grace, though, I will be so."

"Thomas, you—!" Again he didn't let her finish. After thoroughly exploring her mouth, he kissed down along her throat and chest.

She plunged her fingers into his hair when he took her nipple into his mouth again. He circled and flicked at it with his tongue, nipped gently, then rubbed to soothe the small burn. Fire ignited deep inside her, making her squirm and arch, straining toward him, desperate for some answer to the building need. She knew not what the answer might be, only that he would have it.

A hand moved down over her belly and nudged her legs apart again. He stroked her quim with gentle fingers, finding the sensitive, secret places that made her jump and squeal when touched. Each breast got its share of his attention as well while he explored her cleft. One finger worked its way into the opening of her womb. Another searched and rubbed until he found the bud that formed the center of her pleasure.

Juliana sobbed and moaned as he worked on it, rubbing faster and harder, bringing her to a tension that made every muscle in her body hard. The incredible pleasure built until she didn't see how her body could contain it. A knot tangling inside her grew tighter and harder. It had to burst. Yet still the need grew greater and greater as he worked her, sucking at her nipple and fingering her quim.

Finally, when she was sure she'd die if something didn't happen, the knot unraveled in a giant explosion that drew a shrill scream from her. Shudders ripped through her that jolted from head to foot. Pleasure beyond anything she'd ever guessed possible filled her.

Sir Thomas held her while the spasms continued. They gradually calmed to occasional jolts of smaller release, leaving her feeling as though she floated on a cloud, somewhere closer to heaven than she could imagine being. Yet for all that, it felt incomplete. She needed him closer, inside her. It couldn't be, though, and she appreciated his restraint.

He seemed content just to hold her as the jerking eased and her breathing returned to its normal rhythm. As marvelous as the pleasure had been, an even more profound contentment spread over her as she lay in Thomas's arms, with him stroking her hair. Nothing would ever feel better than this.

The serpent of guilt soon intruded into the Eden of her pleasure, however. She had no future with him. She was deceiving him, and whatever kindness he might now feel toward her would soon turn to anger and scorn. It took every bit of will she had to keep the tears from falling. Her mouth might have shaken a little, too, but he could surely take it for the aftermath of passion.

She sighed deeply. "Thomas, you are indeed a master instructor. No one has ever taught me anything of such moment as that."

He brushed her hair back and kissed her. "I've never had so apt a pupil." The stars lit in his eyes when he laughed. "In truth, I've had very little practice, so I suppose I'm fortunate to have a pupil of such talent as to disguise my shortcomings."

"There are none to disguise. You have played my body as though it were a harp and you a master harpist."

"'Twas indeed an interesting and delightful tune I wrung from you."

Juliana rolled over to face him. "Can you sing such a song yourself?"

"Merely caterwaul."

"May I, then, attempt to draw those unmelodious squeals from yourself?" She pushed at his shirt, driving it up his chest.

"I never *squeal*, my lady."

"Sigh or moan or groan or pant or sing as you will, my lord." Another tug on the fabric and the shirt slipped over his head. Juliana sighed in admiration of his chest, with its strong muscle, smooth skin, and light coating of pale hair. She ran her hand over it and watched the pleasure brighten his face.

His nipples peeked out from amidst the forest of hair, beckoning her to explore and play with them. Her fingers kneaded a soft groan from him.

"Sweet music from you, my lord," she said, leaning over to kiss him. He stared up at her with sparkles glowing in his bright, blue eyes. Love and yearning filled her heart past her ability to contain it, and tears threatened again. To keep him from seeing it, she moved to kiss down his throat to his chest, much as he had done to her. He jerked and gasped when he touched his nipple with her tongue.

It felt so wonderful to give him pleasure, as good as it had felt to have it done to her. No doubt it would be better yet could they be joined as one in it, but that right they did not have as yet. Perhaps never would. Once he learned what she had done, he would not want to see her or talk to her again. Juliana desperately wished she could put the past and future out of her mind. Only that moment existed, and in that moment, she could bring him joy.

She ran a hand over his stomach and down his legs, but his leggings impeded her investigation. It took several tries to get them peeled down. Her eyes must have widened. She couldn't help but stare at him.

He noticed and laughed at her expression. "My lady, you've been married, so you've surely seen a man's cock before."

She had to touch it, run her fingers down it to assure herself it was real. He smothered a groan when she did so. "None so big as this, Sir Thomas. Groswick was not... His cock did not rise and grow as yours has... 'Tis not this size always, is it? 'Twould be uncomfortable."

"Nay, it does not remain always this large. Your presence inspires it to grow and stand to your service."

The tears sprung out before she had a chance to control them. Before he could see, she turned her attention back to his cock. At least her voice remained reasonably steady when she said, "'Tis a goodly length to stand to attention."

He jerked and groaned when she cupped her hand around it at the root and ran her fingers up it to the tip, marveling at the satiny smooth skin there. A bead of moisture stood at the end. She touched it and spread it over the hard shaft.

Below his cock, the hairy balls invited her to cup them in her hand and squeeze gently. It drew an even louder groan from him.

"This pleases you?" she asked.

"It does." The words sounded stretched with the effort it took to get them out.

"Tell me what else to do to please you."

"You're doing quite well now."

"Oh." She stroked up and down his muscular thighs, noting the contrasts between the hair-roughened flesh there and that over his balls and cock.

She loved to watch the jerks and heaves of his body when she touched him, and the way his face drew up in a strange frown of intense pleasure. She felt enlarged herself, as though by giving this to him, it returned to her as a gift.

His breath grew shorter and quicker and a throb raced through his cock.

"Juliana." He had difficulty bringing the words out. "If you do not...stop now, I will not be able to...control myself."

"Why must you control yourself in this, Thomas? You gave me the gift of release. May I not return it to you?"

He watched her for a moment before he nodded and leaned back, closing his eyes as she pumped her hand up and down his cock. She leaned over and licked one of his nipples, drew it into her mouth and sucked on it. His moan was almost a sob.

The throbbing in his cock grew faster, and she tried to move her hand in pace with its rhythm. She could barely keep up though. Within moments, he seemed to freeze in place, his muscles stiff with tension. Then he let out a cry of ecstasy, and his seed spurted from the end of his cock, smearing on his belly and her hand.

He pulled her against him so she lay half on top of him while his breathing slowed to a more normal pace. He stroked her hair and murmured how beautiful she was.

His heart thudded beneath the ear she had pressed against his chest. Juliana wished she might never have to move from this spot, that time would stop and let her remain in that moment of peace and love forever. Each word he whispered to her burned into her heart. He spoke of a future she knew was impossible, a sweetness that would soon turn sour, a love that would shortly become hate.

Chapter Eight

Sir Thomas rode out of the castle with both Ralf and Bertram accompanying him the next morning. He planned to spend the day talking to anyone he could find with cottages in view of the road. Someone had surely seen Lord Groswick leave the previous year. With some luck, he might have a start on tracing the lord's route.

Even before he was outside the walls, Thomas had the strange, prickly sense that unseen eyes watched him. Once on the road beyond the barbican, he stopped for a moment to look around, particularly behind him. He listened, but the only sounds were the normal ones of human activity in the bailey, birds singing, and the breeze ruffling the leaves and limbs of trees nearby. In the distance to the left, he recognized the rhythmic clopping of a hoe being wielded.

"Is there a problem, my lord?" Ralf asked.

"Nay. I thought I heard something odd, but I think now 'twas my imagination."

Ralf gave him a dubious look but didn't comment.

He'd picked a good day for this trip. The sun beamed down on them from a clear, blue sky, making it unusually warm for so late in the year. It might be the last of such days they'd see for a while. The breeze held a hint of winter to come. Ralf's smiling face and shining eyes reflected some of his own joy at being abroad in such glorious weather.

Of course, some of Thomas's joy might be a holdover from the previous night. Had there been any doubt in his mind, it was now expelled. Juliana would be his lady. As a widow, she could make her own choice, and though she was reluctant to acknowledge it as yet, she would soon come to accept that Groswick was dead and she was free of him. It would speed the process if he could find certain proof of the lord's demise.

A few hundred yards down the road, they passed the first cottage and stopped. No one appeared to be around at first, but as they dismounted, a young woman emerged from the cottage, holding a baby on her hip. Her eyes widened at the sight of a knight in chain mail approaching. She eyed the sword at his hip warily. For a moment he feared she might panic, run back inside, and bar the door.

Sir Thomas sought to reassure her. "If you please, Madame, we mean you no harm. We merely have a question or two. No harm will come to you or your child, no matter what your answer be. I have no quarrel with you or yours."

The woman still hesitated but she didn't run away.

"I'm Sir Thomas of Carlwick, Madame. The king has sent me to inquire into the fate of Lord Groswick. I'm sure you're aware that he's been gone for nigh onto a year. His current location is unknown and we fear something dire might have befallen him."

Her expression didn't change much, though she relaxed a little bit and set down the child, who toddled off to explore a pile of twigs on the ground nearby. "I knew Lord Groswick had gone, my lord, and that he hadn't returned."

"Did you see him leave? Surely his party went right by here as it left."

"Perhaps they did, my lord, but I didn't see them. Nor did anyone here. 'Twould have been remarked on had any of us seen him pass."

No doubt that was true. It would be a very big event in their lives to see the lord and his entourage pass by.

"We've talked about it a number of times," she continued. "We were surprised to learn he'd gone and we'd not seen a thing. With the noise they make, 'tis hard to miss."

"Know you if any of your neighbors, or anyone around here, did see them go?"

The woman shook her head. "None saw him that I've heard, my lord. I'm sorry."

"Thank you for your time anyway." At his nod, Bertram handed her a coin.

The woman looked startled, then grateful. "Thank you, my lord. Good fortune in your search."

But good fortune seemed determine to elude them. The next stop produced the same result: the residents remembered neither seeing nor hearing the passage of Lord Groswick's company. They, too, admitted there had been much speculation on that fact when it was learned he was gone.

Twice while on the road, Thomas felt that same prickly sense of being watched. Each time he stopped to scan the area around, but he found nothing to account for it.

Just after midday, they came to the village closest to the keep and stopped there for refreshment and information. Of the two, refreshment was far easier to find.

A small tavern sold passable ale and decent bread rolls. Sir Thomas's appearance drew a great deal of interest. A pair of giggling maids vied for the honor of serving him. The ale flowed freely as they brought pitcher after pitcher until Ralf and Bertram broke out in laughter each time one of the serving girls approached.

He had to take the arm of one maid to prevent the deposit of another pitcher none of them needed. "No more ale," he said. "But if you have a moment, I've a question for you."

The girl's eyebrows rose and then she blinked several times at him before her face broke into a wide grin. "Of course, Sir Knight," she answered.

"Do you remember when Lord Groswick set out from the keep to go to the Continent? 'Twas almost a year ago now."

Her smile faded into a disappointed frown, but she did consider his question. "I was told he'd left, but I don't remember seeing it."

"Would he likely have come through here?"

She blinked flirtatiously. "'Tis the most direct way to the main road toward London, so 'tis likely enough."

"But you didn't see him. Did anyone you know?"

Again her forehead wrinkled as she considered the question. "Nay, my lord, now that you ask. I don't believe anyone I know has ever said they saw him. But I'd ask Master Roger." She glanced toward the man running the tap on the keg in the corner. "If anyone knows 'twould be him."

But it appeared no one did know. Master Roger didn't, though he was willing to expound at considerable length concerning possible routes Lord Groswick might have taken, the lord's churlish temperament, the variability of the weather, the difficulty of procuring grain at reasonable prices, and his body's fluxes. Before he left the man, Thomas asked, "Did Lord Groswick have any enemies that you know of?"

Master Roger stared at him for a moment before he shrugged. "No actual enemies that I know of. But few friends. He was not a man who endeared himself to others. Some lords can be strict and fair, but still be personable enough in themselves to earn respect and loyalty beyond the demands of duty. Lord Groswick was not such a man."

It took Sir Thomas a while longer to extricate himself, though he had gleaned enough useful information from the conversation. It added sufficient weight to prior observations and growing doubts to tip suspicion over toward conclusion.

Absolutely no one had seen Lord Groswick leave the keep, a very strange thing, indeed. A baron with a company of knights and men-at-arms made a noisy and colorful party that couldn't help but attract attention. How might Lord Groswick have left with no one at all noting his passage?

And then, other than his wife, no one seemed particularly concerned that Lord Groswick had apparently vanished. Barons were not often popular among their own people, but in this case, all he'd heard suggested no one honored or respected the man at all. Many had mentioned Groswick's bad temper, stinginess, and a general churlishness. In fact, he'd heard not one good thing about the man since his arrival, or even before. Though the king was concerned about his absence, he'd never mentioned any personal care for the man himself.

If he guessed right, Lord Groswick had not left the keep, or at least not left the area. Which meant he was either dead or in hiding. Groswick hadn't inspired the kind of loyalty in his people that would allow him to remain long in hiding with no one betraying him. Nor did there appear to be any motive for him to absent himself from his keep and comfortable life.

If he were dead, though, why had no one reported it to the king? Juliana might be concerned about her future prospects, but she had too much honor to let that stop her from doing her duty in the situation.

It made no sense.

They made two more stops on their way back to the keep, but those yielded no more information or clues.

The sun sank below the tree line just as they approached the barbican. The gate began to screech as it opened for them.

The sound must have hidden the click and snap of the crossbow firing. It almost drowned out Ralf's sudden cry, but Thomas happened to be riding close by and heard it. He swung around to look at the squire.

The boy swayed on the horse and would have fallen off had Thomas not caught and supported him. He didn't have to look far to find the cause. A crossbow bolt protruded from the young man's left shoulder.

Bertram joined them and steadied Ralf's nervous mount while Thomas pulled the boy across to sit in front of him. The squire's eyes were wide and startled, but his expression pulled into a frown of pain.

"Hold on," Thomas implored Ralf. "We're not far from the keep. There's help for you there."

Ralf nodded. His face had paled alarmingly, and his breaths came out in loud pants, but no blood dribbled from his mouth, a good sign that the wound might not be fatal.

"Bring the horse," Thomas shouted to Bertram, then kicked his mount into a canter toward the gate. It stood almost half open, but Thomas ducked under it rather than wait.

He yelled, "To me, to me," as he rode into the bailey, stopping in front of the steps to the main door.

A crowd gathered and willing hands helped support Ralf while he dismounted. "Carry him inside," he told a pair of men he recognized from his sessions of arms training.

As they entered the hall, several servants came running toward them, followed by Lady Juliana herself. "Take him to my quarters," Thomas told the men carrying Ralf.

"What happened?" Juliana asked. "What is wrong with him?"

"A crossbow bolt. Again."

Juliana stopped and went pale. "Oh, no!"

Thomas regretted the harshness of his words. "Juliana! We need your help. Do not faint on me."

"I never faint," she answered. "I'm very strong." She grimaced. "Oh, dear, that was not worded as it should have been. Rather, I try to be strong. At times, though, it seems all the strength in the world wouldn't be enough."

"You manage under difficult circumstances better than any lady I've ever met."

"Thank you. I do what I must. How badly is he hurt?"

"The bolt is in his shoulder. High. More than that I cannot say."

She nodded and called to one of the servants nearby. "Gwen, go fetch William Barber. I fear we'll need his services." The young woman nodded, turned, and raced the other way down the corridor.

They arrived at the door of Sir Thomas's quarters, just as the two men lay Ralf on his side on the bed.

They had to cut away the squire's leather jerkin and shirt from around the protruding shaft. The bolt had entered his left shoulder very near the armpit and gone through at a sharp angle, so that the triangle-tipped front emerged below the collarbone nearly under his chin. It had mercifully missed his neck. Blood seeped from the injuries on either side.

Juliana winced, but probed around the wounds on either side. Ralf gasped and flinched several times, though she tried to be gentle and avoid jostling the shaft.

"No blood is coming from his mouth," she said. "I believe that is a good sign. And I cannot feel any bones misplaced. Can we keep the wound from going morbid, I believe he should survive this."

She put a gentle hand on the young man's forehead. "Hold on a few moments, and we'll have you put right. I'll get you something to help the pain as well."

"'Tis not so bad. I can bear it," Ralf answered, through clenched teeth. His pale skin, shallow breathing, and tense frown belied the bravery of the words, however.

Juliana turned to another of the servants gathered round to see what was happening and standing ready to help. "Avice, go fetch some of the pain infusion I make for my mother. And the salve for wounds. Sarah, clean linens." Both girls acknowledged the orders and departed.

Lady Ardsley came into the room as the girls left, leaning heavily on her cane. She looked even smaller and more frail than she had just a couple of days ago. Her expression turned grim as she surveyed the area, and saw Ralf's injury.

Juliana turned to look at her mother. The younger woman's expression changed briefly, turning from grief to something darker and grimmer, with a hint of determination and possibly challenge.

Lady Ardsley saw it and grew even paler, were that possible. She shook her head, but said nothing.

William Barber, a large man of middle years and gruff manner, arrived just then, distracting everyone's attention to him. He took a quick look at the young man. "'Twill be best to cut off the tip at the front, then pull the bolt out the back," he said. "We'll have to slide it forward some first, though." The tip just barely protruded from skin, not far enough to be easily cut off as it stood, but far enough that it would likely cause more damage should he try to pull it out from the back. William turned to a boy who'd run along behind him and asked him to get some tools.

With Sir Thomas, Bertram, William, and Juliana all steadying him, they shifted Ralf to make it easier for William to reach the arrow from either side. The squire gasped a couple of times as he was moved.

"Now, hold him very steady for me," William instructed. "Sir Thomas, and you there,"—he pointed to Bertram and another man watching—"Get on the other side of him and don't let him move when I push. My lady, keep his head lifted and well away."

The men got in position, holding Ralf steady. William pushed the shaft forward into the wound, forcing the tip further out from his chest. The young man gave a short, sharp cry when the bolt moved, then clenched his teeth together hard and was silent.

"There, 'tis done." William released his hold and looked around for the boy he'd sent off. The youngster arrived at that moment, holding a saw and grippers. "Bring them here, lad."

William took the saw from the boy and moved around to Ralf's front. Before he started, he redistributed the men around the squire to hold him steady.

It took several agonizing minutes to saw the head off the bolt. William had difficulty maneuvering because the tip was still so close to Ralf's body, just below his face.

Still steadying his head and trying to keep it out of the way, Juliana took Ralf's right hand and let him squeeze hers. Tears ran down her face, but she said nothing, and held on firmly. Because he couldn't bear to look at Ralf or the work on the arrow, Thomas instead watched Juliana.

Her gaze focused on Ralf, and the combination of compassion and determination in her expression struck Thomas to the heart. Juliana was everything a man could want in his lady. He could scarce believe his good fortune to find her, and now, when she should be free to make her own decisions about her future.

After a minute or two of William's sawing, Ralf suddenly let out a sharp cry and went silent. Thomas looked at his face. His squire's eyes had closed and his expression smoothed out. Thomas must have made some outcry because all looked at him.

Juliana tried to offer a reassuring smile. It mostly failed in that effort but her words succeeded. "He's fainted. A mercy. God keep him so until we're done."

In that much, at least, God was merciful, and Ralf didn't waken. William worked faster with the squire unconscious, and soon had the head off the shaft. Then he switched sides again to pull it free of the young man's body.

Blood poured from the injuries both front and back. William and Juliana cleaned them both, spread the ointment Juliana had sent for on them, then bandaged them as tightly as they could.

They turned Ralf and settled him on the bed. Servants volunteered to keep watch on him through the night. The rest of the household retired. Before they left, Juliana and Thomas both requested they be notified if there were any change in Ralf's condition.

Since Ralf occupied Sir Thomas's bed, Juliana somewhat shyly invited him to share hers. He was too tired to do more than drop into bed and fall asleep immediately, but in the few seconds between lying down and drifting off, Thomas realized again how much he loved having her in his arms, snuggled against his body. He found so much to admire in Juliana beyond her beauty: her strength, courage, compassion, fairness, and a sweet sense of humor. It had taken him long years to find his lady, but she more than justified the wait.

Chapter Nine

Though it felt wonderful to be tucked into Sir Thomas's arms and nestled against his warm, strong body, Juliana had a difficult time falling sleep. She lay awake for a long time, rolling over and over in her mind what to do next.

She couldn't let the charade continue. Poor Ralf had nearly been killed today — and might yet die — in a murder attempt that was likely aimed at Sir Thomas and was surely intended to help keep her secret. Her efforts to prevent any more violence on her behalf had failed. There was only one way to keep anything more from happening now. If Sir Thomas knew her secret and went immediately to the king with it, it would eliminate any reason for murder.

That didn't solve the problem of her mother, however. Would Thomas allow her to remain here long enough to see her mother's last days lived in peace and comfort? Would the time it took him to get to the king and return be long enough? And could she keep from her mother that Sir Thomas knew? Her mother hadn't much more time and Juliana desperately wanted that time to be peaceful and free of worry. The thought of losing her mother made the tears start again, though she tried to keep her weeping as quiet as possible to avoid disturbing Thomas.

She would tell him as soon as she reasonably could, beg him to forgive her and give her the time she needed, and offer her promise she would face whatever consequences arose from her actions. Would he take her word, after the lies she'd already told him, though? In truth, so long as they didn't torture her, she could face the thought of death. It seemed a fine irony that she should have that shadow hanging over her now, when she'd finally found the sort of love, sharing, and companionship she'd looked for in marriage.

It would hurt him to know she'd lied, and to have to report her guilt to the king. She hated she'd done that to him. She'd put him in a horrible position of having to make his report to the king or sacrifice his sense of honor to save her.

After a while she fell into a restless doze.

Near dawn, a knocking at the door woke her. "My lady," a man called from beyond the door. "My lady."

She pushed aside the bed curtains to see that one of her ladies had answered the door and was speaking with the man. After a moment, the maid came back to her. "My lady, Wendell says that Ralf is half-awake and thrashing around in pain. They beg you to come."

Juliana stood and let the maid help her into her wrapper.

Sir Thomas also stirred. "Find my man, Bertram, and send him to me," he requested of the maid.

Juliana nodded for her to do as Thomas asked. She hurried across the corridor to the room opposite.

Ralf moaned loudly as she entered. His eyes were open but glazed, and his pale skin showed spots of high color on each cheek. As she approached the bed, he shouted something and an arm swung wildly.

"Keep him still," she ordered the woman sitting with him. "We don't want the bleeding to start again."

Between them they held Ralf down to the bed. Thomas came in and assisted them. Juliana put a hand on Ralf's forehead. "He has a fever, but 'tis not too high as yet." She moved a hand away from the bandage on his chest and breathed a sigh of relief. "No bleeding again here." Thomas helped her roll him far enough to let her ascertain no fresh blood stained the bandages at his back either.

Two other servants came into the room to check on Ralf's condition. Juliana sent one of them to fetch more medicine, while asking the other to fetch a basin of water from the well, and then relieve the woman who'd been sitting with Ralf for the past few hours. Together she and Thomas kept Ralf still while they waited for the others to return.

"Is this bad?" Thomas asked.

The concern in his tone was another knife to her heart. He cared for his squire and worried about him. "'Tis expected that he would run some fever. If 'tis just reaction to the wound, he should get over it well enough. A bigger concern is that the wound turn morbid. Should that happen..." She couldn't bring herself to say the words. "But I've put a salve on it my mother taught me to make. She swears it has kept many an injury clean and helped it heal. We can only wait and see. But his youth and good health work in his favor."

Thomas sighed and nodded. "I'll be off as soon as he's settled. I want to go look at the place where the bolt was fired to search for clues. I will find out who did this thing."

"And then?"

He shrugged. "You are the lady of the keep. 'Tis for you to say what punishment might be appropriate."

"Do you find him, we'll discuss what punishment would be suitable."

"I will find him," he said, the statement so harsh and confident, she couldn't doubt it was true.

A servant arrived with the water, followed rapidly by another with the medicines Juliana had requested. Juliana took a cup and gave Ralf an infusion meant primarily to bring down fever, then, using a spoon, she gave him a few drops of the tincture of poppy to relieve his pain and help him sleep.

A short while later, his attempts to thrash around stopped and he eased into sleep. By then the sun had risen and its light poured in the window.

Thomas breathed a loud sigh of relief. "Will he sleep for a while?"

"Aye, most likely."

"Good. I'll take my departure then. I want to get out where it happened before others trample the ground and no possible sign remains of who fired the bolt."

Juliana stood up and moved toward him. "Take care out there. 'Tis likely whoever fired that bolt intended it for you. And they may well try again. When you return this evening, we must talk. There are things I need to tell you." Ralf groaned in his sleep. "Later."

He leaned down and kissed her. "Send word to me if he…"

"I will."

The rest of the day was fairly quiet. Juliana sent someone to ask Peter Randolph to come to her, but by evening he'd failed to respond. She spent most of the day on routine jobs, but stopped in to see how Ralf fared every hour or so.

Thomas returned in the late afternoon, looking tired and discouraged. His expression suggested he didn't have much success, but she hadn't the opportunity then to question him except briefly. At the time he came in, Ralf was stirring again and moaning in pain. In addition, his temperature had started to rise.

"I've sent for more of the pain infusion for him," she assured Thomas when the knight frowned over his squire. "Did you find any signs of who shot him?"

"Nothing," he admitted. "There were no footprints, signs, or anything else to help. No one saw anything. Though we were in sight of the keep walls, the bolt was fired from the woods between the road and the hillside. I—"

Ralf kicked the covering off and waved an arm around, nearly knocking over the cup on the table nearby. Thomas helped her hold him still again while they waited for the medicine to arrive. The squire's skin felt very hot and beads of perspiration stood out at the young man's temples.

"Is this bad?" Thomas asked. "He feels much hotter than this morning."

"Aye, he does. 'Tis normal that he should run some fever following such an injury. We can only hope he can come through it."

"What do you think?" Thomas asked.

As much as she wanted to reassure him that the young man would soon be well, she couldn't in all honesty. "I believe that as young and strong as he is, he should be able to survive it. But only God can say for sure what will happen."

The second dinner bell sounded.

"I doubt not you're hungry," she said to Thomas. "I'll stay here with Ralf for a while. When you go down to dinner, would you ask one of the servants to have a tray sent up to me? Ask for more cool water to be sent up as well, if you please."

"Perhaps I should stay with him while you go down. You're no doubt in need of a respite yourself."

"Nay, 'tis better I stay. I want to watch the medicine and its effect on him. There may be need to give him more, but it must be carefully measured."

Finally Thomas nodded. The servant arrived with the medicine shortly thereafter. Another dose calmed Ralf, though it took a while, but his fever remained high. Juliana began to bathe him with the cool water every few minutes.

She was wiping the cloth across the young man's forehead when Sir Thomas himself returned with a tray of food. A servant followed him, bearing a basin of fresh water.

Thomas set the tray down on a table. "Let Mary tend him for a few minutes while we eat." He dragged a pair of chairs over to the table and set them on either side of it.

Juliana handed the cloth to Mary, gave her a few instructions, then joined Thomas. He'd brought them each a beef pie with savory gravy and a pitcher of ale. Juliana feared he'd want to talk about his investigation or ask her who she thought might have fired the crossbow, but he didn't. Instead he questioned her about various aspects of running the keep, its history, and the people who lived there.

Juliana breathed a sigh of relief that she hoped he would interpret as exhaustion. She couldn't make her confession here and now. Not in the same room with Ralf and the servants. Not when they were both absorbed by worry for Ralf and grief for his pain.

After a quick meal she returned to Ralf's side, where she planned to stay for the rest of the night or until the fever broke and he began to recover. Thomas spelled her for a while so she could get a quick rest, but she felt so uneasy about the squire, she did no more than doze lightly before rising again to return to him.

For most of the night he remained feverish, sometimes muttering in delirium or waving arms and legs. One of the servants stayed up with her, and the two of them bathed the squire with cool water and tried to keep him from moving, lest he break open the wounds. By morning he seemed calmer and no worse, but no better either.

Thomas again brought her food to break her fast in the morning, and sent her off to bed for a time while he sat with Ralf. He promised to call her should there be any change. She slept longer this time, but still woke feeling sluggish and unrested.

* * * * *

William Barber came in around midday to look at Ralf's wounds and help her change the bandages. Both of them were relieved to find the injuries had closed and, aside from some drainage from the hole in his back, showed little sign of going morbid. Juliana smoothed more salve over both wounds before they wrapped them in clean linen. Still, the boy's high fever worried her, and she continued her efforts to cool him down.

Just after midday, her labor was rewarded and the fever broke. Juliana had noticed that the squire seemed calmer, even when he should be due for another dose of the fever medicine. His color improved as well. When she touched his face, she found it cooler, though still clammy with sweat. She sponged him off and sat by his side, ready to act again should his fever climb. By the time she finished, Ralf had sunk into a deep, peaceful sleep.

Thomas found her dozing in the chair later in the afternoon. His kiss woke her from the light sleep in the nicest possible way.

"He looks better," he commented when he saw her eyes open.

"The fever broke a little while ago. 'Tis not certain it won't return, but it is a favorable sign."

He tugged her gently to her feet and pulled her against his chest. "Thank you," he said. The words rumbled in the ear she had pressed against him. "I can't tell you how grateful I am."

He was grateful now, but how would he feel when he learned the truth? As he would shortly.

Juliana looked up at him. "Do not thank me yet. He's not entirely out of danger." She stopped and gathered her courage. "Thomas, we need to talk. Let me call Mary to sit with Ralf."

He nodded and waited with her for the maid to appear, then they walked across the corridor to her quarters.

"Have you had any success finding who fired the bolt?" she asked him.

He sighed. "None. I questioned a number of people in the keep, but no one admits to knowing anything about it.

It can't be so, but they will not betray one of their own to me."

Juliana took a deep breath and stepped away from him. "Thomas, there's something I need to—"

A sharp rapping sounded at the closed door, followed by a man yelling, "Lady Juliana! My lady! Are you within! Your mother—she's collapsed. We need you!"

She forgot what she was saying to Thomas, whirled, and went to the door. "What has happened to my mother?"

Three people stood there and all began to speak at once.

"Lady Ardsley fell—"

"Your mother had a—"

"She went very pale and—"

With all of them speaking rapidly, at the same time, she was at a loss to follow. "A moment, please. Hush." She looked at the man she thought most likely to give her a coherent answer. "George, what has happened to my mother?"

"She collapsed in the hall, my lady." Even the usually calm George sounded breathless. "We've taken her to her bed."

"Is she awake? Has she said anything?"

"Nay, my lady. Her breathing... It doesn't sound right."

Juliana's stomach twisted into a tight, hard knot. She'd known it would be coming, but she'd hoped not so soon. She wasn't prepared.

"I'm coming." She turned back to Thomas. The compassion on his face almost undid her. After a brief but fierce struggle, she managed to control herself enough to say, "We still must talk, but I hope you'll forgive and excuse me now."

He nodded and came to her, put an arm around her shoulders, and hugged her to his side. "Let's go see your mother."

The walk was a short one of just twenty feet or so down the corridor, but it seemed much longer to Juliana. Only Thomas's arm around her and the strength he lent kept her from breaking down. Even so she held her breath as they made their way to her mother's quarters, dreading what she would find there.

Chapter Ten

Thomas held onto Juliana as they approached her mother's chamber. She trembled so hard, he feared she would collapse without his support. Most likely she wouldn't, though. She'd already been through much and dealt with it. She had a strength to equal the two other remarkable women he'd met, the two his friends had wed. But it pleased him to think he could give her some assistance.

The figure in the bed looked tiny and shrunken. With her eyes closed, skin pale, and features drained of all vitality, Lady Ardsley was just a tiny wisp of a woman. The spark of life burned low in her and would soon flicker out entirely.

Juliana jerked to a halt a few feet from the bed. Her startled gasp turned into a sob before she could suppress it. The sound cut off sharply, though, as she swallowed her reaction.

She finished the journey to the bed and said softly, "Mother?"

For some time nothing happened, though Juliana called softly several more times. Finally, the old lady opened her eyes and tried hard to smile. "Juliana." The word was a harsh, labored croak. "Come here, my love. I'm going home soon."

"Mother, no!" An unsuppressed sob accompanied her protest.

"Aye. 'Tis time. I'm tired, Juliana, and the pain… The flesh is…too much of a burden. I'd be quit of it. I only want…" Lady Ardsley had to take a moment to catch her breath. "I have one more thing."

The woman turned to look at him, and even that small movement cost her effort and pain.

"Sir Thomas." She let out a small sigh. "May I speak with you?" She glanced at Juliana and the servants in the room. "In private? For a moment?"

"Of course, my lady." He nodded for the servants to leave.

Juliana hesitated, her features twisted into an agonized frown.

"I'll not let her over-tax herself," Thomas promised. "And should she…get worse, I'll call you immediately."

Finally Juliana sighed and nodded. "A moment or two only, please, Thomas."

"A moment or two only."

She left the room, her normally light, quick step, slow and heavy.

Lady Ardsley watched him steadily. A small, fragile spark animated her features as she reached out painfully, groping for his hand. He took hers and clasped it. It felt like holding a bundle of bones.

"Sir Thomas."

He moved closer to the bed, groping for the chair and moving it with his free hand. He sat. "My lady?"

"I am at the end of my time. I would ask a favor of you."

"If it's in my power, my lady, whatever you will."

"Juliana," Lady Ardsley answered. "When I'm gone...she'll have no one. None to take care of her."

"She seems well able to care for herself and those who depend on her."

The dying woman shook her head. "It seems so, but, truly...Thomas...she needs someone. Love and companionship. She has suffered much. More than you know. And she is so alone."

Again she had to pause to gather her strength.

"You care for her," the lady said. "I've seen it. And she cares for you."

"Aye," Thomas agreed. "It should rest your spirit to know I would make her my wife, should the king approve. I have no reason to think he'll refuse."

A small smile curved the thin, pale lips. "Aye, it gladdens my heart. But..." Her chest rose and fell several times before she spoke again. "Your oath, Sir Thomas. That you'll take care of Juliana. Would you swear it to me?"

The request stunned him so much, he took a moment to answer. What she asked involved a considerable responsibility, yet it was not much different from the promises he hoped to make to Juliana herself in the form of wedding vows. "My lady, if it gives you ease, I'll do so."

She gripped his hand tighter. "Please, Sir Thomas. Swear on your honor as a knight...that you'll guard and care for Juliana all the...days of your life."

He put his other hand on top of hers, so that her small, frail fingers hid between his much larger ones. "My lady, I swear to you, on my honor as a knight, that I will protect and care for Juliana to the best of my ability, so long as I live."

Lady Ardsley tightened her grip on his hand, a gesture of gratitude, he thought. The desperate worry in her expression eased to peace and contentment. She sighed lightly as she relaxed. "Thank you, Sir Thomas. You…give my spirit peace. Take joy in…Juliana. With my blessing."

Her eyelids slid down, but then rose again more slowly. "Send Juliana to me now, if you will. But, if you please, do not tell her what…you've promised."

"As you wish." He stood up, gazing down on the slight figure. The animation had once again drained from her features. "May your soul rest in God, my lady."

Thomas left the room. Several servants loitered in the hall. Two of them returned to Lady Ardsley's quarters at his nod. "Where is Lady Juliana?" he asked the woman who remained.

"With your squire, my lord."

"How fares he?"

"I know not, but when I looked in—"

She broke off as Juliana opened the door and joined him in the corridor. He met her fearful glance and nodded to indicate her mother yet lived. Relief softened her expression. Thomas glanced toward the door through which she'd just exited.

"He improves, I believe," Juliana said, seeing his anxiety. "The fever has not returned. His sleep is peaceful and his heartbeat is strong."

Her expression quizzed him, but she didn't ask what her mother had wanted.

"She's resting," he said. "She seems at ease."

A man rushed along the corridor toward them, long black robe flapping around him. "Father Samuel," Juliana said. "I'm relieved you're here."

"Your mother, my lady?"

Juliana nodded.

The priest bowed to her and then to Thomas. The man's ascetic features showed genuine concern as he pulled a bottle of holy oil from a pocket of his cassock. Thomas followed Father Samuel and Juliana back into the dying woman's room, watching as the priest gave Lady Ardsley the last rites, anointing her with oil and praying over her. When he asked for them all to join in prayer, Thomas knelt beside Juliana.

Once they concluded, he excused himself to check on Ralf. He found the young man sleeping peacefully, guarded by a tired servant who snapped to attention when Thomas entered. The man relaxed but showed a bit of guilt.

"Has he awakened yet?" Thomas asked.

"Nay, my lord, though he has stirred once or twice. I think 'twill not be long before he does."

"Go rest a while," Thomas ordered. "I'll sit with him. Should Lady Ardsley grow worse, however, return forthwith so I may be with Lady Juliana."

The man nodded, rose, and departed.

Thomas sat in his place, watching Ralf sleep. The squire stirred occasionally and even muttered once or twice. As it wasn't the hysterical raving of delirium, nor did it suggest any discomfort, Thomas made no attempt to quiet him.

The peace and quiet gave him time to think about many things: his relationship with Juliana and the future he hoped for with her; the mysterious assailant; Lord Groswick's disappearance; the attacks on him and Ralf.

The warning bell for dinner roused him from his considerations. Since no one had come to him, he presumed no changes had occurred in Lady Ardsley's condition. But when the manservant returned to relieve him, Thomas went back to see if there was any news.

Juliana and two female servants sat in chairs surrounding the bed, but the dying woman lay still and unmoving. They all looked up at him as he peered in the door. Juliana beckoned him to enter.

"She's sunk into a deeper sleep. Her breathing is slowing and her heartbeat is weak. I fear she may not wake again." Only a small break on the word "fear" betrayed Juliana's grief. Her expression was set and controlled, her eyes dry but shadowed. He wished he could embrace her, hold her against him, and let her draw on his strength, but he hadn't the right. Yet.

"Shall I bring up some dinner for you?"

Juliana looked surprised. Sunk in concern for her mother, she'd either not heard the bell or hadn't considered eating. "I don't believe I could eat."

"You need to keep up your strength. Too many people depend on you."

She nodded, and he went downstairs to collect food and servers. When he returned, he enlisted the help of the other two women in the room, neither of whom had any qualms about eating, to persuade Juliana to consume a small trencher of venison stew.

Later he tried to convince her to retire to bed for a few hours rest, leaving him and the servants to watch with her mother, but she refused. Even his promise that they'd send for her should there be any change failed to get her to go. He sat with her for a while instead.

Lady Ardsley's breathing slowed and grew shallower throughout the night. It stopped completely just as the sky began to lighten.

Juliana leaned over to kiss her mother's face and held onto her hand, her shoulders heaving as sobs she could no longer control finally overwhelmed her. After a while Thomas moved to her side and gently drew her to her feet.

"She's gone. Come with me." He led her out of the room.

A crowd consisting of most of the household waited outside. Many of them had been there all night. He nodded to let them know it was over. William Randolph led the others into the room as Thomas drew Juliana out. He felt sure Randolph would do what was necessary now.

He carried Juliana to her quarters, kicked the door shut behind him, and sat on the side of the bed, cradling her in his arms. She buried her head in his shirt while she wept. Folds of cloth on either side of the shirt were bunched into her fists where she held on tightly. Her body shook and the dampness soon penetrated the fabric over his chest.

She cried in near silence, broken only by the occasional louder sob. But the tears flowed hard enough and long enough to soak most of the front of his shirt. Thomas held her firmly and brushed a hand through her hair in an attempt at comfort.

He fought back a few tears of his own, both in sympathy with Juliana's sorrow, and in a more personal regret for the passing of Lady Ardsley. He'd liked the old lady and hoped her soul now rested with the Lord.

Juliana's weeping continued for a long time. It didn't surprise him. She'd kept a lot of grief contained within her, and it needed to come out now. He made no attempt to stop or calm her, but sat quietly, struggling with his own feelings. Holding her so felt more right than anything he'd ever known before. How long would he have to wait before he could decently talk with her about their marriage?

After a while, her crying wore down to a series of hiccupping sobs. "I got your shirt wet," she said, her voice wavering from the effects of prolonged weeping. "I'm sorry."

He laughed softly. "You've naught to regret. I've added some moisture of my own."

She looked up at him, startled. She reached up and wiped a tear from his cheek with a finger, then studied it for a moment. Her face twisted, and he feared she'd break down again. "I've much to regret. But now is not the time."

The words puzzled him, but when she sighed and relaxed against him, he didn't want to disturb her by asking what she meant. She snuggled closer. Her breast squeezed into his chest, its softness a rousing pressure on his flesh. He kissed the top of her head. He wanted to kiss every other inch of her, but this wasn't the time. Instead he allowed himself to indulge in visions of a future together, possibly here, or possibly somewhere else, depending on the king's will.

When he roused from the reverie, the calm rhythm of her breathing indicated Juliana had drifted off into sleep. Carefully, so as not to rouse her, he eased her off his lap and back onto the bed, arranging her head on one of the pillows. He stood beside her to straighten her legs, then he walked around the bed and lay down beside her. He slid into sleep as well, though it didn't last long.

The angle of sunlight coming in the window when he woke told him he'd slept no more than a couple of hours. Juliana still lay in the position he'd set her in. She'd had no rest for two nights running and needed this sleep, so he rose carefully, moving slowly to avoid jarring the bed. He changed clothes quietly and eased the door shut when he left the room. He found a servant out in the hall and asked that a guard be set outside the room to ensure Juliana would not be disturbed before midday.

The servant watching over Ralf looked up and nodded to him when Thomas peeked in at that door. "He woke earlier," the woman said softly. "He wanted a drink. I got it for him and he went back to sleep." Thomas glanced toward the bed. Despite the bandages and his pale complexion, the young man looked better.

Thomas left the room, went down through the great hall and out into the bailey. The weather had changed considerably since his outing with Ralf and Bertram. Winter now tried to chase away the lingering pleasantness of fall. Clouds obscured the sky, and the wind had a raw chill to it, suggesting cold rain or even snow approaching.

Choosing people at random, he questioned those who passed by on errands, asking them about Lord Groswick, when he left, what people thought of him as lord, where they thought he might be now.

Two people were so intimidated by him they managed to give only one or two-word answers that told him little. A third person stuttered too badly to get out more than a few words altogether. But another two did answer questions, and their uneasiness in responding began to solidify his coalescing suspicion. Groswick was not only dead, these people knew he was, and for some reason, they wanted to hide the fact.

Had he died of a normal disease or an ordinary accident, the word would surely have been passed on to the king. Even if they wished to remain under Lady Juliana's rule, they would have known it wasn't possible. Had Groswick died of some shameful illness such as leprosy that might have brought quarantine on them? More likely, save that he saw no sign anyone here suffered from such a thing. Plague, perhaps? But the pestilence spread with such virulence, the keep would have been much less populous.

Another, more likely possibility occurred to him. Perhaps, Groswick did still live, but was mad. 'Twould make sense they would try to conceal such a thing. But where might they have secreted him? Somewhere in the keep, for a certainty.

Thomas walked around the bailey, considering various possibilities, ducking into occasional recesses in the walls, looking into shops large enough to have back rooms. In the walls he found only storerooms for arms, grain, lumber, nails, and other supplies. The back rooms he peered into generally served as sleeping quarters for apprentices or as storerooms.

He studied other features of the main building, but saw no obvious wings or outbuildings he couldn't account for.

As he had the other day while out riding, Thomas got the feeling of unseen eyes watching him. It made him wary, remembering how that day had ended. But no crossbow bolts soared his way.

The sound of voices and a clanking of shovels or other tools led him around a wall on the far side of the keep. As he rounded the bend, he realized the wall beside him was part of the chapel. A group of five or six men worked in the area beyond, digging. Rough wood crosses stood up from the ground at intervals, with a few stone markers in a row near a rock wall at the back. The men labored just beyond the farthest of them, excavating a new grave. For Lady Ardsley, no doubt.

He didn't want to interrupt their work, so he stopped and watched for a moment, scanning the area. A few other places showed the disturbed dirt of recent burials, some where fresh patches of grass had just begun to sprout.

The men didn't notice his presence or chose not to acknowledge it, if they did. But someone else did.

His alertness kept him from being startled or unprepared when footsteps sounded from behind him. Their quiet, halting approach suggested some attempt at stealth, or at least wariness. Thomas waited until the person was within a few feet, then ducked to the side, whirled and shot out a hand to grab the arm of the man behind him.

The man let out a startled cry. "Sir Thomas!"

He was a very young man, familiar, but it took Thomas a moment to place him. "Peter Randolph? Never sneak up behind a knight. You could find your head separated from your shoulders before you had a chance to identify yourself."

The young man paled. "I'm not... I didn't..."

"I can see you have no weapon drawn, and well for you 'tis so." Thomas released his hold on the young man, who stumbled as he tried to back away. "What might I do for you, Randolph?"

"Naught." The word wavered a bit. The young man drew a harsh breath and struggled to control his voice. "Naught. I just wondered...about Lord Groswick. Do you know any more of what has become of him?"

Thomas relaxed himself but considered his words before he spoke them. "I have some idea, but no clear picture. And nothing to prove what I suspect. I'm going back inside. Walk with me, if you will."

Randolph nodded and turned with him back toward the main door to the keep.

"What do you believe happened to Lord Groswick?" Randolph asked.

Thomas stared at the younger man, studying his eager expression. It was there, not so much in his look as in his words. An undertone of challenge he surely didn't realize he let sound. Randolph knew.

"Groswick never left the castle," Thomas stated. "I know not whether he is dead and buried here, though I suspect 'tis the case, or if he be immured in some remote cranny to hide his madness or a shameful disease. But all I've learned convinces me he never left. Did you actually see him go?"

Thomas watched the young man's face carefully as he deliberated about what to say. The fact that it took him so long to decide was all the answer Thomas actually needed.

"Nay, my lord. I didn't see him go. I'd been sent on an errand to the miller at Hoopsdale at the time, however."

"Aye. It appears everyone had business elsewhere on that day."

Randolph remained silent for a few moments before he asked, "What will you do, my lord?"

Thomas shrugged. "What can I do? Until someone will tell me the truth, I have naught but suspicion to take to the king. How he might choose to act on it, I cannot guess."

They climbed the steps up to the great hall, where Randolph left him to go in search of his father. Thomas went back to his quarters.

Ralf was awake and propped up on pillows. Though pale, his eyes were clear, and his expression had a spark of vitality and alertness. Thomas sent away the servant who'd been sitting with the squire and settled in to talk with the young man for a while.

Chapter Eleven

Juliana roused slowly, aware at first only of a peace she knew was too fragile to last. No one else lay beside her in the bed. Gradually memory returned. Her mother was gone. Her own confession to Sir Thomas had been interrupted by her mother's collapse, but it still loomed before her. Not today, though. She had too much else to bear today.

She rose and rang for a servant to come help her dress. From the angle of the sunlight, it had to be near noon. She never slept so late, but exhaustion had overtaken her when she'd finally cried herself to sleep in Sir Thomas's arms.

There was much to do. She forced herself to drink the tea and eat the slice of toasted bread the servants brought her. Her stomach wanted none of it, but she dared not let her strength wane.

Sir Thomas was out in the bailey somewhere, she was told when she inquired about him. A quick stop in to see Ralf found him sleeping peacefully, with no trace of fever. He roused a bit when she put a hand on his brow, mumbling something at her, but not waking fully. "Sleep," she told him as she left.

Her mother's body had been removed to the chapel. Two servants accompanied her there, carrying the things she would need to prepare Lady Ardsley for burial. The procedure should only have taken an hour or so, but because she had to stop frequently to control her emotion, it was almost mid-afternoon before she finished.

The priest came in as Juliana was completing the preparations. Along with the two servants who'd come with her, they said a rosary for the repose of her mother's soul before they discussed arrangements for the funeral mass in the morning.

Once that was done, Juliana went on to the kitchen to ensure they could lay out extra food for the mourners the next day.

On her way back through the great hall, a group of people led by Peter Randolph stopped her.

"He knows, my lady," the younger Randolph said, his voice low but angry. "He knows, and he'll report it to the king if we don't stop him now."

"What does he know?"

"He knows Lord Groswick did not leave the keep."

"But he doesn't know of Groswick's fate?"

"Nay, though he strongly suspects. He'll take his suspicions to the king, and the king will act."

"Then so 'twill be," she answered. "Perhaps 'tis time and beyond for this to be set right. I'll not have him or his people hurt any further. My mother is beyond worrying about consequences, and my soul is sick of the stain of deception."

"Your mother is beyond your care, but what of the rest of us?" the maid, Avice, asked. "We need you as well. And what of the king's retribution should he learn of the deception? We've lied to protect you, my lady. Will you now betray us by exposing those lies?"

It stopped Juliana for a moment. "You've none of you done other than what I ordered or requested, and should I have to answer for my deeds to the king, I'll make that clear. The responsibility is entirely mine, and the consequences shall be also. The king will not fault you for following the orders of your lady, as is your duty to do. As for you needing me... There are others here who can maintain order and keep things running smoothly in my absence. The king will appoint a new lord, and I feel sure Sir Thomas will see that our new lord is better than the former one."

"Yet you cannot assure us of that," Avice argued. "And you've done well by us, lady. What happened was no evil on your part. We would not wish you to suffer for it."

"I'd prefer not to suffer for it either. Yet, I fear if I do not at least own to my guilt and pay for it in this world, 'twill be worse for me in the next."

"Then you will tell Sir Thomas?"

"Aye. I would have already had not my mother fallen ill."

"My lady, I beg you — "

They were all so engrossed in the confrontation that none of them noted the arrival of the man who stood in the arch — until he spoke. "I would very much like to learn what confession you have to make, my lady. I presume it concerns Lord Groswick's mysterious disappearance?"

Several of them whirled and gasped at once, a few others squealed or murmured, "Sir Thomas!"

Juliana had a moment of dizziness and disorientation while it felt as though the floor beneath her wobbled. She groped for a table nearby and leaned against it as she fought for control.

While struggling not to faint, she managed to miss a piece of action, though she heard the sound of a scuffle, raised voices, yells, squeals and the thunk of a fist on flesh. When she could risk straightening and turning to look, she realized that several of the man had surrounded and overcome Sir Thomas. They now held him tightly, a man on either arm, pinning them back behind him, wedging him between them to keep him still.

Peter Randolph held a long, wicked-looking knife, and as she watched, he raised it to the knight's throat. Juliana had no doubt of what he intended.

She screamed, "No!"

It froze them for a moment, long enough to let her throw herself between Sir Thomas and the knife. Peter took a step back but didn't lower the weapon. "Drop it, Peter," she ordered.

He hesitated. Watching his eyes told her he planned to try to move around her. "Drop it now, before I step forward into it." She said it with so much force that several of the people around screamed and surged forward to stop her. She held out a hand to halt them.

Peter looked dumbfounded and his breath came out on a sob. "My lady!" He slid to the side and so did she, then she moved forward. The young man dropped the knife hastily before she could impale herself on its point.

She felt and heard movement behind her and turned in time to see Thomas free himself from the two men hanging onto him. But others rushed in and pinned him once again.

"No," she ordered, seeing Peter reclaim the knife and approach. "I'll not have it. He's done nothing to harm us. He merely seeks the truth."

"He'll harm you if he learns the truth, my lady," Avice said.

"He'll learn the truth now. I'll have no more lies. There have been too many already."

"My lady," several people protested.

"Nay." She shook her head to deny their protests. "Release him."

The men holding Thomas looked uneasy. One let go but others continued to hang onto him. Peter's hand tightened around the knife, and his expression grew more determined.

"If you harm him, I'll go to the king myself and tell him all."

"My lady, you cannot," Peter insisted.

"No more lies. I cannot live this way. Too much harm has been done already. I'll tell my story and take whatever consequences may come. Sir Thomas—" She turned to face him. "I rely on you to ensure the king understands whatever guilt there is here belongs to me alone. These people must not be punished for my actions."

She dreaded meeting Sir Thomas's gaze, but stiffened her will and did so anyway. All the anger and betrayal she expected brightened his eyes.

"What happened to Lord Groswick?" he asked, ignoring the men holding him as though they were no more than flies lighting on him.

"I killed him."

For several long, unbearable moments, he just stared at her. Shock and astonishment kept him still. Her words took time to penetrate beyond his surprise, and even then they had to burrow into his awareness before he started to comprehend. Belief took a few minutes longer. "Tell me all," he demanded.

Juliana breathed out on a long sigh. "I will. But not here."

She drew herself up and looked around at the crowd that had gathered. "I am still your lady," she told them in her most authoritative voice. "Release Sir Thomas. Take Peter Randolph into your custody instead." For a moment she feared they might not obey so she added, "Now!"

The men acted. Randolph protested as the knife was removed from his hand, and the two men who'd held Sir Thomas wrapped up the young man's slighter form instead.

"My lady, please!" the young man pleaded. "I was trying to protect you."

"I know that. But I told you more than once I wanted no harm to Sir Thomas and his people. You did not listen or obey. Now I cannot trust you."

She turned to the men holding him. "Remove him to one of the dungeons until I decide what to do with him. I'll not have a guest in this place go in fear of his life during his stay here."

The men did as she ordered and dragged off a protesting Randolph. Juliana turned to the others present and asked them to return to their work, reminding them that her mother's funeral would be on the morrow. When they'd dispersed, she nodded for Thomas to follow her to her quarters.

As they entered the room, she tried to read his expression, to gauge how he felt about her admission. What would he do when he heard all of it?

She sighed, grieving for what might have been. If she'd been the innocent, sorrowing widow he'd thought her. If she hadn't been persuaded to hide the truth. If she hadn't argued with Groswick that day. If her life had worked out along different lines. If she'd married someone else…

What might it have been like if she'd married Sir Thomas instead of Groswick?

"The story," Sir Thomas said, once he'd closed the door behind them. "The truth this time, if you please."

She nodded, but initially her voice refused to work. Something clogged her throat, making it difficult to force the words out. She drew in a long breath, letting it out on a sigh.

"You never met Groswick, so you would not know what he was like." She paused, not sure how to frame her explanation. "He was not a kind man. Nor an honorable one like yourself. He had no patience. And when he was angry, he had little control of it. If events didn't go as he wished, he was as like to strike out at what he saw as the cause of his frustration."

She watched Thomas, but still couldn't read anything from his expression.

"He often struck out at others. The entire household was terrified of him." She drew another breath, trying to calm herself. "Within a day or two of our wedding, I was also. Unlike you, Sir Thomas, my Lord Groswick had difficulties with his manhood. It often refused to rise to his desire. I did all I knew how to rouse him, but more often than not, I failed. He faulted me for being unable to inspire him. Indeed, at first, I did believe it was my lack. But then I learned he'd approached most of the presentable women in the area, and none had been able to draw more reaction. More, I discovered he… But, nay, he's dead now and 'tis best not to speak of it."

"In any event, as I said, he blamed me for his failure. He beat me for it." She stopped to control a sob that tried to escape.

"The scars on your face?" Thomas asked.

She still could tell nothing from his expression. "Aye. I learned early to allow him to do as he would. Once, just months after our wedding, I called for help. A servant came and tried to protect me. Groswick killed him. Beat him to death. My mother tried to talk to him, and when that failed, she tried to stop him, but he paid her no mind. He even pushed her once and made her fall. Between his mistreatment of her and the servant, I learned not to argue, to be as silent as I could when he…struck me."

She closed her eyes for a moment, unable to bear the pain of the memories. "One day, about a year ago, we argued. As usual, I hadn't been able to rouse him, but he had also lost his favorite horse a few days before, and had…other things go wrong. He was more than normally frustrated, which roused more than normal anger. He accused me of…many wicked things. I would accept his berating me for not being able to rouse him, though I'd come to doubt the fault was truly mine, but when would have me…meeting other men on the side and cuckolding him with the stable boys, I refused to accept it. We fought. He slapped me and pushed me. When he began to hit me with his fists, I…panicked. I feared he would kill me, so I fought back. I tried to run away, but he barred the door and chased me around and around the room. When he caught me again, I picked up something — a pitcher — and hit him with it. He reeled back from me. There were things on the floor — cups and dishes and candleholders — because we'd upset a table. Groswick tripped on one of them and went down. He fell on the table that was overturned. He hit his head on a corner. Hard. So hard it... It split his head open. I believe he died almost immediately."

Juliana found herself shaking almost uncontrollably. Her knees wobbled so badly she had to sit on the side of the bed before she fell down. She didn't expect any comfort from him, and he didn't offer any. She did anticipate recriminations, but those didn't come either.

"Why didn't you just go to the king and tell him Lord Groswick had died as a result of an accident?"

"Because I killed him. I hit him with the pitcher and he fell."

"You need not have told the king that."

It took an effort to hold back her sob. "I was not thinking clearly at the time. I was...upset. In truth, I was so blindly distraught, I knew not what to do. My mother, Master Randolph, and a few of the others came in and saw what had happened. 'Twas they who decided to bury Groswick and put it about that he'd left to fight on the Continent. I should have stopped them, but I didn't think to do so then. I was unable to think at all then. I only just survived. By the time I recovered enough to reason it out, 'twas done, and I saw no way to undo it without further harm. In truth, I never thought it would cause any injury. I supposed eventually the king would realize Groswick was gone and appoint a new lord and all would be well."

He didn't say more when she paused.

"Then you came and turned everything upside down. I never thought anyone would inquire so deeply into what had happened to Groswick. Nor did I expect I would ever meet a man I would come to...admire and love so much. I feel as though I've been torn in two over the past sennight since you came. I could not think what to do, but I knew I could not allow you to be hurt. It grieves me more than I can say that Ralf was injured. And my soul feels as though it has a great stain on it from the lies...and from what I did to Groswick."

Her head felt so heavy she could barely hold it up. Her whole body sagged with weariness, grief, sadness, and a looming sense of defeat. What would he do now? He stayed so quiet. She dared a quick look up at him.

He wore no expression she could read. His eyebrows drew together into the start of a frown, but otherwise he looked more sad than angry. He shook his head, from confusion rather than negation, she thought.

"Your actions did cost a man his life," Sir Thomas finally said. "Yet it appears that was more accident than intent. I cannot believe you meant him any harm. You sought only to keep yourself from injury. I could not condemn you for that, yet I cannot say with any certainty how the king might view it."

He sighed heavily. "In truth, it concerns me more that you mounted such a deception to hide the truth. It seems to magnify your guilt, and pile definite wrong on possible wrong. I understand 'twas not your doing at first, yet later when you came to reason again, you did not stop it when you might have. It has dragged everyone here into the deception with you, and almost cost Ralf his life."

The words were quiet, almost devoid of expression, but she felt each one as a dagger to the heart. She couldn't deny the truth of his indictment, so she accepted, embracing the pain as part of her penance, knowing she deserved it.

"You know how I feel about lies and deception," he continued. "Lies tore apart my life once and nearly destroyed it. It seems I'm destined to be once more devastated by a woman's deception."

Her heart broke. She'd heard that term before, but had never guessed one could feel such a real, clenching pain in the chest. The desolation and regret were almost past bearing, but even so they were overshadowed by the knowledge of the pain she caused him. "Sir Thomas," she ventured in a wobbly voice. "I'm more sorry than I can ever tell you. I know 'tis easy to say, and you have no reason to believe I'm being truthful now, but it is the truth. I regret my actions more than you can imagine. If I had the opportunity to go back and change them, I assure you I'd do differently." She sighed, heartsick with despair. "You will not believe it, but I have been wracked with guilt, and would have confessed the truth to you shortly, had you not learned of it on your own. In fact, I was about to tell you all when the message came about my mother's collapse."

One sob she couldn't quite suppress leaked out. He looked so shocked, so stricken, so stunned. Despite her fear for herself and the pain she anticipated, she couldn't help but curse herself for causing him such anguish. There was nothing more she could say in her defense, so she waited quietly for him to pronounce her doom.

Instead, for a long time, he said nothing. He paced the room, occasionally turning to look at her, but he remained quiet, thoughtful and frowning.

Finally she could stand it no longer. "What will you do?" she asked.

He halted his step, though he continued to look at the far wall of the room rather than at her. "I know not. I'll have to think more on it."

Chapter Twelve

Thomas felt as though he'd been punched in the gut and then beaten over the head with a club. Why had he not guessed this? Now that he knew, it stared him in the face, how obvious it had been. Who else would own so much loyalty from the people that they would lie continually and without fail to protect her? He'd been so close to the truth. He'd guessed Groswick was dead and the people of the keep concealed the truth. Why had he not made that final leap and realized how few reasons there were for such a far-reaching deception?

Yet there was no point now in berating himself for the failure, which might, in truth, have much to do with his feelings for the lady. The only pertinent question that remained concerned what he should do about it. For that he had no answer.

If he took her now to the king, how would His Majesty view her actions? Did he dare expose her to the possible harshness of the king's condemnation? Yet, if he pleaded privately on her behalf, he thought it likely he could gain some mercy. Surely he could make the king understand she'd truly intended no harm, and just tried to protect herself.

Did he want to plead with the king for her? He looked over at her, sitting on the bed, looking so fragile and defeated. Aye, he wanted her still, despite the lies she'd told and their nearly fatal consequence. Whether he should have her was a separate issue entirely. How could he contemplate a future with a lady who had lied so? Could he ever feel secure with her or find the trust in her a man should have in his wife? Did he dare believe her words of repentance and regret?

He didn't want to take her to the king. Yet if he didn't, what did that say about his own sense of honor and the vows of fealty he'd given? How could he live with himself if he did not tell the king the truth? Yet he'd given a vow to Lady Ardsley as well, to protect and care for Juliana. How could he honor both vows?

The dinner bell interrupted his painful musings. He had no answer, for himself or for her.

"We should go down to dinner," he told her. "I have not yet decided what to do, and may, perhaps, take some time before I can see my course clearly."

Juliana nodded and stood. "I don't believe I can face dinner this evening. Perhaps I'll just retire to my quarters."

He stared at her. "You're no coward, my lady. This night, I think your people need to see you. They know you grieve, and they know you're in a difficult situation. Will it not encourage them to see you eat and drink with them? Would you have them think I've harmed you or so demoralized you that you can no longer function?"

She considered his words and finally nodded. "You are right. They need to see me." She straightened herself and, with a visible effort, composed her expression into something calmer if not exactly serene.

Duty, he realized. Juliana understood duty, especially to the people who depended on her. Perhaps part of the reason for her deception was from duty to them. She'd said they'd created the deception without her knowledge or will. If that were so, she had likely faced a conflict of competing demands similar to what tore him apart now. Could he believe someone who'd lied to him, though?

She stopped at the door, squaring her shoulders before she turned back to him. "Sir Thomas, before we go down, I must say this. This morning I unburdened my soul to Father Samuel and received God's absolution, but that does not relieve me of facing the results of my wickedness. I know that I did wrong and I'll answer for the consequences. I'll go with you to the king for his judgment on the death of Lord Groswick, though I beg you for a few days to see my mother laid to rest and arrangements made for my absence."

She sighed heavily. "I also owe *you* my repentance for the lies I told and the pain it caused you and your squire. For that I'll also accept whatever punishment you feel it right to impose. In truth, I believe what I did to you the greater evil. Groswick died, but I never intended it should happen and would not have ever considered doing anything deliberate to bring it about. But I did deliberately lie to you about what had happened, knowing it was wrong. Worse, I let you...nay, I *led* you into wanting me too much. I regret it all, save that..." She drew several heavy breaths before she regained control. "What we did together was as sweet as anything I've known in my life. But I had no right to it. And I had no right to tempt you to want it, too. I am an evil and wicked creature, but I know my wrong and I hope in time to right it, if...if circumstances allow. Please, Sir Thomas, I hope someday to have your forgiveness. To gain that, I'll do whatever penance you ask of me, accept whatever punishment you deem fit."

He couldn't sort out all the emotions and thoughts roiling through his head right then. He still wanted her with desperate intensity. He wanted to believe her, wanted to believe she meant her protestations of repentance, but she had lied in other things, just as Margaret had lied. In fact, lying had been a way of life for Margaret. How could he know that it wasn't so for Juliana as well? Yet, Margaret had never once acknowledged any fault in herself nor accepted any correction for her sins. He couldn't imagine her ever making the speech Juliana just had. Perhaps there might be a way for him to learn the truth of this lady.

"I'll consider what you say," he answered. "For now, though, I am too confused and still too shocked to answer properly. However, there will be time to lay your mother to her rest and to arrange affairs here. For the moment, that's all the promise I can give you."

She nodded, accepting it. Her eyes were huge and still a bit red from tears, while her lips were ripe and swollen. The delicate, floral scent of her soap teased his nose. He wanted to kiss her so desperately it was an ache in his groin and his heart. He wanted her in his arms, her breasts pressed against him, her quim throbbing at his touch.

Before he could act on the impulse, however, she nodded, said, "Of course," and turned to leave the room. She carried herself with her normal regal dignity. Only her somewhat slower step and more solemn expression betrayed her pain.

Dinner was a somber affair, devoid of the normal jesting and laughter he'd become accustomed to. Instead people spoke in low, hushed voices. Many of them made a point to stop in front of Lady Juliana's place to offer regrets and condolences on her mother's passing. Juliana picked at her food but did manage to swallow some. Thomas himself ate, but only because he'd had little other food that day and his body simply required it. He found little pleasure in it, even in the savory roast duckling and honey-laced bread pudding.

When the meal concluded and they rose to go, he headed back toward his quarters, where he could sleep on the cot Ralf had used before his injury. Juliana hesitated for a moment in the corridor, as though undecided whether to come after him or proceed to her own quarters. When she chose, wisely, not to follow him, he didn't call her back.

The next morning dawned cold and gray. By the time they'd gathered in the chapel for Lady Ardsley's funeral mass, a damp snow had begun to fall. The solemn service moved him almost to tears. Sobs and sniffles sounded from every corner of the chapel, especially during the priest's brief words on the joys awaiting them all in heaven, the joys to which Lady Ardsley was surely now party. As they marched out for the graveside prayers, the snow increased. Larger flakes fell faster and harder, gathering in the freshly dug hole and on hats and cloaks. The wind blew his clothes around and pushed strands of hair into his eyes. Many of the people crowding around still sobbed aloud, though Juliana had remained mostly calm throughout.

Thomas felt frozen almost completely through by the time they retreated back into the great hall where food and blessedly warmed ale and mulled cider awaited them. As some folks sat to eat, while others rushed back and forth bringing food and wine, the scene reminded him of the day he'd arrived and the bold way Lady Ardsley had questioned him. He understood now that simple curiosity alone hadn't motivated that catechism. Still, something about her sharp good humor and zest for life, even as her body failed, had touched him. Apparently others felt the same. Many stories of Lady Ardsley were recounted as they ate and drank.

Though she had come to Groswick fairly late in life, the lady had made a home for herself and been well-liked by the people. Thomas gained insight into why, when a couple of the stories recounted ways the lady had tried to intervene with Groswick and even maneuver him into doing things he didn't want to do. At one time, she'd gone toe to toe with the lord on a question of meat distribution and somehow won a bigger allotment for the workers on the estate. The lady had mediated a dispute between Groswick and the local miller that threatened the flour supply of both keep and crofters.

She'd also held strong opinions on a number of subjects and had no hesitation in voicing them whether asked or not.

Thomas couldn't help but watch Juliana as she listened. She smiled at some of the funnier stories and cringed once or twice in embarrassment, but for the most part she seemed composed but solemn. She accepted the condolences and pats on the shoulder from those around her with dignified, but warm gratitude.

Some of the stories about her mother amused him, until he remembered the vow he had made to her on her deathbed. The lady had found a way to manipulate him even from the grave, though his own feelings about Juliana would have dictated little difference in his actions. He still hadn't quite decided what those would be.

Eventually, the gathering broke up, and people departed to use what remained of the day for work. Outside, the yells of children playing in the first snowfall of the season occasionally leaked into the building. A quick glance convinced him he'd have to wait at least a few days before he could leave to go to the king. The blanket of snow was already several inches deep, with flakes falling harder than ever.

Thomas sighed as he watched the white fluff dance on the wind. The odd, floaty motion of the flakes drew his eyes to follow them. Peace rode on their lacy shoulders as they fluttered and drifted downward. If only he could find some of the same peace. Perhaps if he were wiser and could judge the situation more accurately, he might find it. He shrugged and went to see how Ralf fared.

He found the squire sitting up in bed, complaining about the thin beef soup a servant spooned into his mouth. Seeing that, Thomas felt confident, for the first time since his injury, of Ralf's full recovery.

"You need the strength that soup will bring you," he told the irritated young man.

Ralf shook his head. "There's nothing here to give me any strength. 'Tis naught but flavored water. Can I not at least have a bit of bread to sop it up with?"

"You've been ill for some time. Your system needs time to adjust to taking nourishment again."

"My stomach insists it's more than ready."

Thomas had to grin. He looked at the servant. "I don't see that a bit of bread could hurt. Perhaps if he eats most of the soup, it would be possible?"

The servant shrugged. "At your command, my lord."

"Eat," he told Ralf.

The young man did, and when the bowl was near empty, Thomas asked the servant to fetch some bread for him. While they waited, Ralf questioned him about what had happened during his illness. The servant returned with the bread just as Thomas finished relating Juliana's confession, with some of the more personal parts edited out. Ralf had no trouble filling in the gaps, of course, but he waited until the servant had left the bread before he asked, "Will you take her to the king?"

"I don't know," Thomas admitted. "I don't know how the king might react, and I'd hate to see her treated harshly for what was, in truth, an accident."

"You could tell the king Groswick had an accident."

"Aye, I could. I could even reconcile it with my conscience. But I'm not sure it's truly the right thing to do."

Ralf nodded. "Do you still want to marry the lady?"

He started. "Scoundrel! What makes you think I would want to wed her?"

The squire just grinned. "I've seen the way you look at her. The only other lady I've seen you look at that way was Lady Mary. And I remember you told someone she's the only lady you'd then met you would consider marrying, save that she was already wed to Sir Philip. But the way you look at Lady Juliana is even more...even stronger than the way you looked at Lady Mary."

Thomas conceded the point. He couldn't hide much from Ralf's sharp eyes and even sharper intelligence. "Aye, I love the lady. And I would still marry her, save that I'm not sure that's the right thing to do either."

"Because she lied to you?"

"Aye."

"But she did it to protect others as well as herself. 'Tis very understandable she should do so, and I'm certain that until we arrived she had no idea there was any risk of harm to others."

"True," Thomas admitted.

"The real question, then, is do you think she'd lie again, should similar circumstances arise?"

Ralf did have a way of cutting through the emotional clutter to reach the heart of an issue. Thomas sighed as he considered. "I don't know, but I think not. I think she has learned something of the dangers of lying."

"But you still doubt you can trust her sense of honor."

"I suppose I do," he admitted. "But perhaps..." For the first time, he saw a possible solution to their dilemma. It wasn't without risk, but he thought the king would listen to any plea he made for mercy for her.

"You see a way out? I hope so, in truth. I like the lady, and I think she would bring you happiness. I hope..."

"What?"

Ralf blushed and looked embarrassed. "I hope someday I'll meet a lady as beautiful and...good as she is, who'll like me as much as Lady Juliana likes you."

"You will," Thomas said. "You already attract ladies like flowers attract bees. You're tiring."

Ralf had started to slide down, and his eyelids drooped as he reached the end of his energy.

"Rest now," Thomas said. "I'll not be going anywhere in the next few days. It's snowing, and there's a deep coat on the ground already."

Ralf nodded but was half asleep by then.

Thomas retired to a corner of the room where a small writing desk provided work space. Since he could do little else, he wrote several letters to friends and family, telling them where he was and in a general way, what he was doing. He would take them with him when he left and find a messenger later to deliver them.

Since most people had eaten heartily earlier, only a light dinner was served. With the snow outside, there was little else to do, so most people attended, though conversation was subdued in deference to Lady Juliana's feelings. The lady was quiet as well, and somewhat distracted.

When it was over, Thomas started to follow her to her quarters, but changed his mind before she had time to notice his intent. He knew what he wanted to do, but needed to put more thought into how to present and organize it. The day had been long, and his exhausted mind required sleep and more time to sort out his thoughts. He went into the quarters he'd shared with Ralf. Bertram was there, sitting with the squire, who slept quietly. The man helped Thomas prepare for bed and settle onto the cot again.

The snow had slowed by the time he woke the next morning, but it hadn't stopped completely. As he made his way down the corridor to the great hall, he stopped at a window to look outside. A few tardy flakes still floated serenely down, adding to the thick white blanket already coating the ground, bleaching the roofs of buildings, and decorating trees with white fluff. The world looked clean and fresh, reborn into purity, yet it was an illusion. The trash and dung remained beneath its white coat, ready to emerge when the snow melted off it.

He reined in his fanciful imagination and went in search of food.

He didn't see Lady Juliana for most of the morning. Two servants he asked hadn't seen her or heard where she might be. One of the men he'd worked with on the training ground invited him to work out with them in a basement chamber they used for the purpose during poor weather. Since his body felt stiff and rusty with disuse, he agreed gladly.

A bell sounding called a halt to the exercises several hours later. Thomas stopped and looked around in surprise. It couldn't possibly be time for dinner.

"'Tis summoning us to the hall for a meeting," one of the guardsmen told him, seeing his confusion.

Along with the others, Thomas wiped sweat from himself and cleaned his sword before replacing it in his scabbard. He met Juliana just outside the great hall and joined her when she beckoned him.

"I'm holding court today," she told him. "And I would have you beside me. 'Tis just a couple of small domestic issues first, but then I have to deal with Peter Randolph. As 'twas you and your squire he injured, I'd have you approve the fate I've decided for him. Though he made an attempt to take your life, he didn't come close to accomplishing it, so I'll not have his life in reparation. I intend to have him flogged, severely enough that he'll remember for a long time, but not so hard as to cripple or permanently injure him."

Thomas nodded. "I will be satisfied with it."

Juliana smiled, but it took an effort, then she drew a deep breath, sighed it out, and turned to enter the great hall. He followed her and took the seat beside hers on the dais. The table had been removed.

The first item of business was a dispute between the smith and a crofter over payment for an item the smith had made for him. Juliana listened to both sides and rendered a compromise decision that gave both sides some satisfaction. Though neither individual was vindicated completely, each seemed satisfied.

The second matter involved a maid who'd been found in possession of several items stolen from others.

After seeing the evidence of the items found in the girl's quarters, hearing from those who'd been with the housekeeper when she'd found them, as well as the original owners of the stolen trinkets, Juliana called the maid before her.

"Again, Jenna?" she asked. "Have you anything to say?"

The girl was crying hard already. "My lady, I try not to take things. Truly, I do. But something comes over me...and I cannot resist it."

"You must learn to resist it, Jenna. You cannot go through life this way." Juliana paused and sighed. "I fear that since four strokes of the rod did nothing to teach you, we must try six this time."

"No, please, my lady," the girl begged, crying even harder. She fell on her knees.

Juliana nodded to a large man standing near the side of the room. He came forward, picked up the weeping girl, and carried her to a bench two other men placed in the middle of the room. They tied the girl's hands and feet to slats in the bench. The big man picked up a branch around three feet long and a half inch thick. Without ceremony, he raised it over his head and whipped it down hard on the girl's rear end. Even though the material of her shift offered some protection, the crack made by the rod as it landed sounded vicious. The girl bucked and shrieked. Five more strokes followed in rhythmic order with a short pause between each. She screamed with each one.

While it was going on, Juliana leaned over and whispered to him, "I truly believe the girl does have strange impulses she finds difficult to control. Yet she must learn to control them or someday she'll face a penalty far worse than a whipping."

When it was over, they released the girl and helped her to stand. She still wept hard as the lictor half-carried, half-supported her over to stand in front of Juliana again.

"Jenna, I do not like having to punish you. I hope you learn from it and will control yourself better in the future. Keep this in mind as a deterrent. The next time you come before me accused of this same thing, you'll receive ten strokes. Do you think you can bear it?"

The girl shook her head tearfully.

"I trust it won't be necessary. 'Tis done now and I'll hear no more about it. Go now. You have the rest of the day off to recover."

The sobbing girl curtsied, buried her face in her apron, and ran from the room.

Juliana sighed again and said softly, so no one but he could hear, "And now for an even less pleasant duty." She called to the men at arms nearby, "Bring in Peter Randolph."

Three guards accompanied the prisoner. The young man still wore the same clothes he'd had on the day he'd tried to kill Sir Thomas, and much the same expression of outrage and anger. They marched him to stand in front of Juliana.

She raised her voice so all in the hall could hear. "Peter Randolph, you are charged with attempting to murder Sir Thomas Carlwick, seated here now. As almost everyone here also was present at the attempt, I see no need to call witnesses to testify to the fact. Have you anything to say for yourself?"

He looked up at her, his expression torn between anguish and bravado. "I sought only to protect you, my lady!"

Juliana's expression remained unmoved. "With an action I had expressly and repeatedly forbidden! I'm sorry, but that argument carries no weight with me." She looked up and around the room. "Will anyone else speak for him?"

As she'd no doubt anticipated, Peter's father, her bailiff William Randolph, stood up. His voice was heavy and somewhat choked. "My lady, my son is several kinds of fool, but there's no malice in him. He truly did seek to protect you, though I know it was against your orders. I agree he must be punished for it, but I do beg that you spare his life."

She nodded to him but said nothing. Instead she looked around the room and finally asked, "Anyone else?"

When no one else spoke, she rose to her feet and looked back at the prisoner. "Peter Randolph, I find that you are guilty of both disobeying your lady and of attempting to take the life of a knight of the realm. As I agree with your father's judgment that your only motive for both was my protection, I do not require you pay with your life. However, I cannot let such wicked deeds go unpunished. Though it pains me to do so, I must order that for disobedience to your lady, you will receive forty lashes with the heavy strap. For the sin of attempting to murder Sir Thomas, you will receive an additional sixty." She glanced toward the large man who'd carried out the maid's punishment earlier. "Martin, take charge, please."

The young man drew a deep breath that sounded suspiciously like a sob, but otherwise he said nothing. He straightened himself up and didn't resist when Martin turned him and led him to one of the pillars that lined the sides of the room, but as he twisted away he met Juliana's gaze with eyes that accused her of betrayal. Juliana didn't react, but sat down and waited, with no expression apparent on her face. Only Sir Thomas was close enough to see that her fingers curled around the arms of her chair with such force the knuckles looked strained and white.

Thomas was shocked and stunned himself. One hundred strokes was a heavy punishment, indeed. Harsher than he would have ordered.

They stripped off Randolph's leather jerkin, but left his shirt and breeches on, and tied his hands to a ring set in the pillar above his head. Martin picked up the heavy strap, a fearsome looking instrument: a strip of heavy leather four feet long by three inches wide, split along a third of its length into two tongues. He wound a few inches of the unsplit end around his hand to anchor it in place and let the rest hang loose until he took up his position behind the prisoner. He flipped it behind his back and swung it around to whip it across Randolph's back. It struck with a loud, painful crack. Randolph's body jerked but he made no sound. In fact, the entire room was eerily quiet, almost as though everyone refrained even from breathing too loudly. It made the whack of the leather against flesh resound even more impressively.

But after a few strokes, Thomas began to understand the wisdom of Juliana's sentence. The punishment was harsh and painful, no doubt, yet in truth it both looked and sounded worse than it was. The strap hit loudly, but it had no edge to tear flesh, and with his clothes to protect him, its bite was blunted. The beating was impressive, painful, and humiliating, yet for all that, it was far from the bloody savagery of some floggings he'd seen.

Nonetheless, he could see the effort it took Juliana to watch impassively. She restrained a flinch several times when a particularly loud crack suggested a more painful stroke. It went on for some time as Martin paced himself, allowing a pause between each lash. One of his assistants marked each stroke with chalk on a slate board and called out the running total after each set of five. Before it was over, a few loud groans and one yell had leaked past Randolph's control. A tear she made no effort to wipe away ran down Juliana's cheek.

A collective sigh of relief rose from the crowd when the assistant called out "one hundred," and Martin put down the strap. Randolph hung limply from his bonds by then, either exhausted or fainting. He would have collapsed when they released him had Martin not caught him and slung him over his shoulder.

"Take him back to the dungeon, but see he has all the care required," she ordered. "I cannot release him until Sir Thomas and his men are away from the keep."

Martin nodded and turned to carry the young man out of the room, but she stopped him, saying, "Let someone else take him back, I have another task for you here."

People had begun to rise and talk among themselves, preparing to leave, but the chatter and movement halted at her words. All turned back toward her to find out what she meant. She waited until Martin had transferred his burden to another man-at-arms, who carried the limp form out of the room, before she spoke.

She stood up and drew a deep breath to steady herself. Even so, her voice wobbled and broke when she announced, "As Peter Randolph has been punished for his attempt on Sir Thomas, I must, in justice, also accuse myself of some part in that crime, for it was my deception concerning Lord Groswick's death that led to it. Knowing the facts as I do, I confess my guilt, and sentence myself to the same punishment Peter Randolph received for his attempt to kill Sir Thomas. Sixty lashes with the strap. Martin, if you will do your duty…" She stepped down off the dais and walked toward the man, ignoring the clamor of gasps, sobs, and protests that broke out from all corners of the room.

Even Martin seemed too shocked and stunned to move. He, as well as everyone else in the room, looked to Thomas. It took a moment before Thomas realized the reason: he was the only one present who could stop what Juliana intended to do. He admired her gallantry and her sense of justice, as she stood ready to accept a severe punishment for her crimes against him, but he didn't want it this way.

Thomas stood up and shouted, loudly enough to cut across the clamor, "Nay, Lady Juliana, I protest."

She stopped and turned toward him. "Why, Sir Thomas? What is your objection?"

Love for her, a love that transcended her beauty and charm, passion that rose from his deep admiration for her sense of honor and courage as well as desire for her luscious body nearly overwhelmed him, but they also helped him find the argument that would win her cooperation. "Peter Randolph is *your* vassal, and thus it is your right to pass judgment and sentence on his crimes. As lady of this keep, you are the *king's* vassal. And as I am the king's representative here, I claim the right to act in his place."

Juliana looked stunned and more than a bit dismayed. "It is true," she said. Bracing herself once again, she added, "I have admitted my guilt. It is for you then, Sir Thomas, to impose a sentence."

"So I shall, and you shall have your punishment. But the right to designate the time and place and method belong to me, and I do not choose to do so here and now."

Her expression changed to a startled frown. For a moment it appeared she might protest, but then she shrugged and said, "As you will, my lord." Around him people cheered and clapped.

She stopped to look around the room, not sure how to react to the relief being expressed. Finally she sighed, shrugged, and said, "We're done here. I thank you for your presence. Return now to your work."

William Randolph sought her out before he left the room. Thomas stood close enough to hear him thank her for sparing his son's life. "He's young, and has much to learn yet," the man said. "He'll grow out of his foolishness."

Juliana nodded agreement. "Let us hope today's lesson helps him understand his folly and the need for more thought before he acts."

They followed others out of the room, but Thomas went with Juliana to the small office. As they walked toward it, he asked, "What did you think to learn yourself from the punishment requested?"

She pondered on that a moment. "I sought no lesson, as I think that already learned, but only atonement."

"You feel the need of it?"

"Aye."

"Your people would not be happy about it. 'Twas clear from their reactions that many of them already carry their own guilt and sorrow for you. 'Twould disturb them too much to see you suffer more, no matter how much you think you deserve it. You shall have your atonement, but in private, administered by me. Go now to your chamber, undress to only your shift, kneel on the floor, and wait for me thus, meditating on your sins."

He saw the flash of fear that crossed her face, followed by acceptance. She wanted to ask what he would do, but hadn't the nerve or thought she didn't deserve to know.

"I'll await you," she promised.

Chapter Thirteen

Juliana hurried to her chambers, threw off her cloak and overgown, removed her leather slippers, and rolled off her stockings. Then she knelt on the stone floor, off the colorful, woven rug in the center of the chamber, to await him. She did indeed meditate on her sins and prayed that somehow they might be granted a way out of this mess into happiness. If not for the two of them together, then she pled for Sir Thomas to at least find peace and contentment. But she couldn't help adding her pleas that they be allowed a future together as husband and wife.

After a few minutes, she began to worry about how long he'd make her wait and what he would do when he arrived. Not so much how he would punish her; she expected him to respect her need for atonement and chastise her well. Rather, she wondered what would come after. Would he turn her over to the king and wash his hands of her? Or would he still want her for his wife? How could he reconcile his conscience with it if he didn't bring her before the king?

Her thoughts made her restless and unhappy, but fortunately he didn't keep her waiting overlong. Because she faced the door, she could watch him enter. A solemn, almost grim, expression set his handsome face in hard lines. In his right hand he held a leather belt and several pieces of fabric that looked like lengths of silk.

"Lady Juliana, stand up," he ordered. The words were stern, untempered with compassion or care.

She got to her feet and stood before him.

"Remove your shift."

She felt her eyes widen and the hot color rise into her cheeks, but she did as he ordered, pulling the shift over her head.

He looked her over dispassionately. "You confessed your guilt for your lies and deception, offered your repentance, and expressed your desire for atonement. I'm here to deliver your chastisement. I warn you, 'twill be harsher than what you would have ordered for yourself. You'll get a whipping with my belt on your bare flesh. No set number of strokes, but I'll continue until I feel it's enough. You'll no doubt think it enough well before I do." He stopped and shut his eyes for a moment, as though fighting through pain. "Do you agree to this?" he asked. "I'll not force it on you if you don't think you can bear it."

"'Tis no less than I deserve," she answered. "I do agree."

"One thing more. You may stop it at any time if you find it beyond bearing. Just tell me to stop, and I will."

She nodded, but part of her wished he hadn't offered her that chance. There might well come a point when pain weakened her resolve and she begged for it to end.

He moved her to stand at the foot of the bed, facing it, and tied each wrist and each ankle to the posts on either side, so she stood spread-eagled and helpless. He fastened another length of silk around her head, over her eyes. She heard the sounds of him walking around, then a moment of stillness, followed by an ominous hiss of leather moving rapidly through the air. But it didn't strike.

Instead he asked, "Are you ready, my lady?"

"Aye, Sir Thomas."

This time the hiss was followed by a loud crack as the leather smacked against her bottom. A jolting shock ran through her, stunning her, but then the fiery burn seeped in behind it. She gasped and wiggled as the sting dug deep into her flesh.

The second stroke came quickly after, lower down on her bottom, painting a ribbon of fire across both cheeks. She moaned as the burn spread into her gut and set her insides aflame. A third stroke dug into the sensitive skin where bottom met thighs.

He continued to pepper her with slaps of the leather on her bottom and thighs for some time. Though it burned with a deep, rending fire, she suspected he wasn't using anything like all the strength of his arm.

She tried to keep still, but her body reacted without her will's consent, wiggling and squirming, trying to avoid the fiery strokes. The silk ties that held her in place didn't chafe the skin, but they held fast and gave her little range of movement. For a time, she had more success in suppressing any outcry after that first gasp.

As each lash laid another painful stripe, she questioned herself for wanting this. She didn't. It was horrible. It hurt almost unbearably. But it was just. She'd sinned, and a young man had suffered far more pain than this as a result. And a part of her rejoiced that Thomas understood and respected her enough to do this for her, and do it properly.

But when the next whack landed harder than previous ones, across the tops of her thighs, all such thoughts fled. It took all her attention to stop a yell from escaping. The burn lit up her skin and worked its way into her blood, spreading all over her body, down to her toes and out to her fingers. The next few were just as hard, and after a few more, she was sobbing and struggling fiercely within her silken bonds.

She jolted in surprise and dismay when he changed direction and lashed the strip of leather across her shoulders. A furious sting broke out in a new place, washing her body with renewed fire. She gasped again and whispered, "Oh, God." It reminded her why she wanted this. A series of *Ave Maria*s and *Pater Noster*s helped her endure the next few strokes, all crossing her shoulders and back, lighting the flesh with blazing pain. Eventually, though, she could no longer concentrate on the prayers.

The leather returned to her derriere, raking over skin already grated and burning. She sobbed aloud, struggling to keep from begging him to stop it. Between that and her efforts to keep from screaming aloud, it took a long time to notice something else strange going on. The deep smoldering burn from the welts left by the strap combined with the fire of each new strike to send heat spiraling into her gut and down farther still. It roused a pressure of need like to what she'd experienced before when he more gently stroked her to climax. Her quim swelled and moisture seeped from it.

Yet it didn't lessen the pain or make the sizzling agony of each stroke easier to bear.

He kept whipping her, moving down her bottom to her thighs and back up again, each lash rousing new fires, jolting her with even more unbearable anguish. The silk blindfold became soaked with her tears. More gasps and even an occasional soft shriek fought past her effort to keep quiet.

Her earlier recognition that he didn't use all his strength was vindicated when he whipped the belt across her derriere even harder than previously. She arched as far as she could within the bonds, and a wailing squeal poured out of her. The fire consumed her, melted her, destroyed all control. "Please..." She stopped herself just short of begging him to stop it.

He heard the words, though. The rain of blows halted. A soft step approached and his breath came loudly. "Please?" he asked. "Would you have me stop it? Do you think you've been punished enough?"

She sobbed and had to clear her throat before she could talk. "Not my will in this, but yours, my lord."

"Ah." That one word held both surprise and recognition, but recognition of what, she couldn't guess.

'Ten more," he said. "But these will be harder. You'll not be able to keep from screaming, so I'm going to stop your mouth. You'll not be able to beg me stop, so I ask you now to say yea or nay to this."

Her breath clotted in her chest as sheer, raw terror poured waves of ice down her spine and along her limbs. She wished she could see his face. Wished she could touch him or ask him to give her some reassurance, some comfort. But that was not for her, not now.

"I agree, my lord."

For a moment, all was quiet, save for the sound of his breathing and hers. Odd, that his seemed almost as ragged and stretched as her own. Then he moved. Footsteps crossed the room and came back.

"Open your mouth," he ordered.

When she did so, a piece of silk was pushed in, and another tied around her head to hold it in place. Bizarrely, it occurred to her to wonder where he'd found so much silk in such a short time.

"Get ready."

She braced herself. But when the leather struck her back, nothing could have readied her to receive it. It was liquid anguish, poured over her and set ablaze. She groaned in agony, but the fabric in her mouth smothered the sound. The bed must have been built solidly and the knots in the silk bonds securely tied. Her wild struggles would have torn them apart otherwise.

Two more strikes across her shoulders felt as though they raked skin from the bone. The fiery burn sent her into a frenzied writhing accompanied by a wild sobbing that leaked past the fabric gag as small squeals.

The fourth stroke, hard across the already raw and burning flesh of her bottom, took her beyond any control. Her scream would have shaken the keep had it not been contained by the fabric. Likewise, she would certainly have begged, pleaded, even ordered him to end it. The fifth likewise felt as though it flayed strips from her derriere.

The next two went across her thighs and burned as though a torch had been laid on them. Pain had her thrashing mindlessly, screaming and praying for it to end.

But she had to endure three more sizzling, rending strokes on her bottom before it was over. By then she had screamed herself out and sunk into exhaustion. The last lash almost didn't register, as though her ability to feel pain was so full, it could no longer function. A strange, floaty sensation had taken hold by then.

She heard, but didn't comprehend, the small clatter as the leather strap was flung against the wall. When Sir Thomas removed the bonds from her wrists and ankles, she would have collapsed to the floor if he hadn't held her.

Her legs had no strength. He held her against his chest as he pushed the sodden blindfold from her eyes with his free hand. She blinked once or twice then stared into his blue eyes, riveted by the depths of love, concern, and compassion there.

"Juliana?" he asked after he'd removed the silk binding her mouth and pulled the soggy fabric out.

The one word held a world of meaning. Was she all right? Could she hear him? Was she overwhelmed? Did she hate him? Want him to leave her? With all the pain, it still brought another hurt to hear the fear in his voice.

She sought to reassure him in the same way. "Thomas. Thank you." She snuggled against him. It comforted her and soothed her aches to feel the warmth of his skin, the clasp of his arms as he held her against him.

He carried her around the bed and settled her carefully on her side. "'Tis done now," he said. "The lies and the deception are behind us. You've paid for it in full and from now it is forgiven and forgotten between us."

The fiery burn of welts across her back, bottom and thighs still ached fiercely, but she nonetheless felt relieved of a burden on her spirit. Not all was removed, but for the moment, her befogged mind could deal with only the one issue. Sir Thomas forgave her and would put it behind them.

She reached out and took his right hand, pulling it in toward her breasts, and holding it there with all her remaining strength. Then she drew it to her mouth and kissed it.

"You should rest now," he said. I'll make your excuses at dinner. Will you need some of the pain tincture to help you to sleep?"

She couldn't help staring at his face, and especially his eyes—so blue, so bright, so full of love and concern. It was a salve more effective than any she knew. "Nay, Sir Thomas, I'll take no medication. I'll rest now, but I beg you wake me at the dinner warning bell if I do not so on my own."

"You needn't, my love. 'Twill be difficult for you to sit."

She smiled at him. "But I must. Half the household will have guessed why we're closeted in my quarters. They need reassurance that I'm neither badly injured nor devastated in spirit." She sighed. "I believe I will require a pillow, however."

He laughed gently, and it did her heart good to see it. "If you insist, I'll sneak in early and set pillows on your chair."

"I would appreciate it. Will you lie with me a while? You surely are in need of a rest yourself, and it would comfort me to have your arms around me."

His smile was like sunshine after a storm. "Aye, if it won't pain you." He walked around the bed and lay down behind her. She was too exhausted and sore to roll or turn to look at him, and though it caused some pain in her back when he slid an arm under her neck, she nonetheless relished the joy of his touch enough to ignore the discomfort.

Chapter Fourteen

Thomas roused to the sound of the dinner bell clanging. Beside him, Juliana stirred as well. A knock on the door followed hard on the warning bell. "My lady?" Avice called. "Would you have me help you dress for dinner?"

"Nay, thank you," Juliana called, without moving. "I can see to it myself."

"As you will, my lady."

Thomas withdrew and rolled over to get out of bed. He turned when he heard Juliana groan softly as she tried to push herself up. Aching muscles and sore skin defeated her first effort to rise.

"Stay there for a few minutes," Thomas told her. "I'm going to put the pillows in place. Then I'll return and help you."

Fortunately no one stopped him or questioned him when he took a pair of pillows from his quarters, noting that Ralf and the servant assigned to care for him both dozed peacefully. He took the pillows to the great hall, slid them onto her seat, and pushed the chair far enough under the table to hide its cushioning.

Juliana had waited for his return. With his assistance, she was able to rise and stand. But when she turned, he sucked in a harsh breath. Had he truly been so hard on her? The evidence stood out sharply on her skin, the marks of the strap a clear map of how hard and how often his belt had lashed her. Her shoulders bore red stripes darkening to bruises in spots, while her bottom was still fiery, the skin grated, with blackish bruises beginning to show. One spot on her left thigh sported a large, heavy black mark where the end of the strap had dug in several times.

"Are you certain you won't change your mind and stay here? 'Twill not be comfortable sitting on that, even with pillows."

"My reasons haven't changed, nor has the necessity. I can bear this."

He suspected she regretted that resolve before midway through dinner, despite the riotous cheers and laughter that marked the meal as the most cheerful one since the night the traveling company had stopped by. But the smiles of the people in the hall and their obvious satisfaction in seeing her at ease and reconciled with Sir Thomas surely compensated for her discomfort. It sent odd streaks of longing into his heart and his groin. All here knew how much they cared for each other, and they just as clearly approved. Yet he couldn't promise either them or her that there would be any future for them, less the one they envisioned and hoped for. As joyous an occasion as it was, he could still see Juliana's relief when all had finished eating. He wasted no time in standing to retire. Perhaps a few realized that the hand he extended to help the lady rise was as much a necessity as a courtesy.

"There should be a bath waiting for us," he said, as they walked the corridor. "I asked for it when I went to put the pillows out. 'Twill do your bruises good to soak out some of the soreness."

The tub sat in front of the fire with two servants pouring buckets of hot water into it. Another pair came in just behind them to add to it. Steam rose from the surface. When a third group of servants had come and gone, Thomas told them it was enough, barred the door, and helped her out of her clothes. He had to suppress the urge to whip himself when he saw how much he'd hurt her. She felt so fragile and delicate as he lifted her over the edge and into the tub that he couldn't believe he'd beaten her so cruelly. No matter that she wanted it, had practically forced him to do it. He'd been harsh with her.

She sank down in the tub, then stopped when the water stung the places on her bottom and thighs where the skin had been grated by the strap. But after a minute she lowered herself the rest of the way. Relief showed on her face as the heat of the water worked its way into her body and loosened tight muscles.

Thomas let her soak for a few minutes, then picked up a washcloth and soaped it. She kept her eyes shut as he ran the cloth over her shoulders and arms. Another pang knifed into him when he found a bruise on her arm in the shape of the end of the belt.

Juliana's eyes opened. She watched him for a moment, then shocked him when she said, "Won't you join me in the tub, Sir Thomas? 'Twill be a tight fit, but I believe there's room enough."

He dropped the wash cloth in his astonishment, but a grin he couldn't suppress spread across his face. He shed his clothes before she could change her mind and climbed in with her. His added bulk pushed the water level almost to the top of the tub, and some splashed out as he lowered himself in, facing her. With space tight, he had to sit with his knees bent, legs positioned outside hers.

They attempted to wash each other, but ended up using the lather from the soap to draw designs on each other's chests. He couldn't keep his hands from her breasts, the sweetest such mounds he'd ever seen or felt. The delicate nipples responded so avidly to his touch, beading into hard pebbles and forcing breathless gasps from her.

"Turn around and I'll wash your hair," he promised.

No doubt she realized that his plans included more than just washing her hair, but she nonetheless acceded, though it took some careful maneuvering in the narrow confines of the tub to shift her without hurting her. She settled against him where she could surely feel the hard jut of his needy cock poking into her back. He washed her hair, massaging her scalp with the suds and sliding it through her long, thick strands. Once he'd rinsed the soap out, he drew her to lean back against him, lifted her so that his legs were under hers, and wrapped his arms around her. He covered her breasts, kneading them gently, caressing the tips. He drank in her soft gasps and sighs of pleasure as he worked her nipples into peaks, which he pressed and pinched lightly.

His right hand left her breast and brushed down over her stomach and belly to her cleft. He nudged her legs farther apart, and pushed a finger into the petals of her quim to part them. She moaned louder when he found her pearl and began to stroke it. Her pleasure built until she squirmed against him and panted with need. He brushed his fingers down the slit, stopping first at the entrance to her womb and exploring the recess there, then going down farther and finding the other opening. She jolted with shock and surprise when he pushed into that entry as well, but adjusted to it after a moment. "My lord," she murmured.

"Is it not pleasant?" he asked

"Aye, it is in a way. But I did not expect anything like it." Her hands wrapped around his thighs, fingers digging into the skin as her tension grew. Every muscle in her body became rigid and hard, her breathing rapid and gasping. She was a knot being pulled tighter and tighter until she vibrated on the edge of climax. He returned to working her pearl with one hand and her nipple with the other, rubbing, stroking, even pinching lightly until her moans grew louder. She shook in his arms, and of a sudden she squealed in startled delight as the spasms of fulfillment rolled through her. While she jerked and panted in the continuing small jolts, he held her against his heart, praising God that he could bring her this pleasure, after he'd given her so much pain. It took a while before she finally calmed and went still.

By then the water had cooled, so he stirred, climbed out, and lifted her from the tub. They dried each other off, though she took a long time about toweling him, and, as before, seemed fascinated by the usually hidden parts of him.

He picked up her shift and went to slip it over her head, but she stopped him. "Thomas, you've pleasured me, but have taken none for yourself. 'Tis hardly fair."

"I've taken pleasure in giving it to you," he answered.

She shook her head. "There's more, is there not? Pleasure is meant to be shared between a man and a woman."

"Between a man and a woman who are married. Do we go that far, I could get you with child, and this is not the time for that."

She considered it. He saw when she reluctantly conceded. "But is there naught we can do to share more fully?"

"Perhaps so. Come here."

Her slight body fit easily into his arms, and her soft curves yielded to his hard angles in a most satisfying way. When he tipped her head back and leaned down to kiss her, it felt as though everything he was, had been, and would be passed to her in the contact. His cock stiffened even more, if that were possible, and strained against her, seeking its natural target.

He kissed her for a while, reveling in the sheer glorious pleasure of it. His tongue roved across her face and into her ear, but took its most vigorous delight in plundering the depths of her mouth. The warm, smooth richness of it tempted him to dig deeper and deeper, to want more and more of her.

Juliana made everything seem brighter, sweeter, more joyful. She gave new meaning and fullness to his life. How could he let her go? How could he risk her, even for the sake of his honor?

When she squirmed against him and put a hand around his jutting cock, all thought fled. He could do nothing but feel. He dragged her over to the bed and lay with her against him. Her hands roved his chest and abdomen, down his legs, up the insides of his thighs and — finally, gloriously — cupped his balls. She kneaded them carefully. His insides dissolved into hot, running fire that made his whole body blaze with wanting her.

He couldn't stand it. The urge, the need, the desperation to bury himself inside her all but consumed him. His hands ran over her hips and then the idea struck.

She stiffened for a moment when he tried to flip her over onto her belly, but it was more from surprise than displeasure. He knelt between her legs, then lowered himself on top of her, letting his cock lie along the cleft of her bottom. Her skin half enveloped him in soft, yielding warmth.

"Does this pain you?" he asked, fearing that he might be causing her sore bottom to ache again.

"Nay," she said on a soft sigh of mixed pleasure and contentment. "'Tis good."

He moved against her, sliding up and down, just as he would if he were inside. He almost spurted right away when she moved against him, trying to match his rhythm. She reached back and slid her hand between his cock and his body so that he was completely wrapped in Juliana.

With her cooperating so completely, it didn't take long before his breath came in pants and sweat gathered at his temples from the effort. Then he felt it coming. He held still, savoring the moment for as long as he could, before the seed poured from him in spasms of release.

He collapsed on top of her, feeling a small whoosh of air as his weight rested on her. He wouldn't remain there long for fear of crushing her or making her bruises ache, but his spirit craved a moment or two of the most complete contact available to them at that time.

After too brief an interval, he forced himself up and off her. He held her in place while he found a towel and used it to clean up the sticky patch he'd deposited.

They lay together, then, with the single candle guttering in its sconce, and drifted on the lazy peace and contentment of their fulfillment. Juliana fell asleep, tucked into the curve of his body with his arms around her. He lay awake for some time, musing on how right this felt, to be protecting her, sheltering her, sharing his life and his love with her. Raw terror shot through him at the thought of losing it, of losing her. He wanted to stay with her here forever, and if they had to fight the entire rest of the world to do it, so be it.

Yet he was a knight as well, and sworn to the king's service. Honor was so much a part of him that if he failed it, he wouldn't know how to live anymore. He'd be nothing to himself and of no use to Juliana. So he'd do what he had to do.

The next morning he rose early, even before the first light of sun brightened the sky. He met a few people coming and going, but none stopped him to ask his business. The chapel was cold and dark, save for the candle that burned on the altar, indicating the presence of the consecrated body and blood of the Lord in the tabernacle.

He knelt and prayed with all his soul and spirit that he be guided to do the right thing, and that all would come out well in the end. He tried to echo the words of the Christ in his prayers. "Not my will be done, but thine." The struggle consumed him, yet when he rose, at last, he found a core of peace settling in his soul.

By then the sun was up and gleaming off white stretches of snow. Already it had begun to melt off some of the tree branches.

He met Juliana in the great hall, where she'd stopped for bread and cider. The lights in her eyes when she smiled dazzled him. The warmth of it ran through him and settled in his heart, expanding it until his chest would barely contain the enlarged organ. And yet it roused a chill as well, a cold frisson of fear for her and for their future.

They sat together at one of the long side tables while they ate, amidst a group of household serfs and vassals. He found peace in listening to the conversation flow around them. The everyday business of the keep had its own rhythm and profound connection to the deeper patterns of life. Its sheer normalcy diverted and refreshed him.

But after they'd finished, he asked to speak with Juliana privately, and they proceeded to her little office. He couldn't help remembering his first interview with her in the room. He'd drastically misinterpreted her reaction to his telling her he thought Groswick dead, yet he'd been so right about the fundamental strength and courage of her. Here she'd first begun to wend her way into his heart. And here he'd have to deliver the news that would test her in ways that would probe her deepest loyalties and honor.

Chapter Fifteen

Juliana braced herself as she watched Thomas work up his nerve for what he had to say. She guessed at some of it already. She'd noted the snow beginning to melt and realized he would be off to the king soon. Would he insist she accompany him to face the king's judgment?

"How soon do you plan to leave?" she asked, when he seemed to have difficulty finding the words to begin.

He drew a sharp breath. His mouth pressed into a hard line, and his eyes narrowed for a moment as though in pain.

"If the thawing continues at the rate it has begun, the roads should be passable by the day after tomorrow." He walked to the window and stood there, looking out. He kept his back to her when he spoke. "I have debated what to do for some time. I will admit there's a part of me wants nothing more than to settle here with you and remain for the rest of my life. I could do so easily and with great pleasure. 'Tis even possible the king would accept it and do naught about it."

He sighed and waited a moment before he continued. "Yet duty and honor dictate I do otherwise. I am the king's man, and I came here on a mission from him. I must return to give him an answer."

The question she wanted to ask stuck in her throat and refused to come out. But it didn't matter. She'd know soon enough in any case.

"I truly believe that Lord Groswick's death was an accident and your own involvement incidental. He died because *he* tried to harm *you*, not because *you* meant *him* any harm. I would swear my belief of that to the king on anything he wished. Yet I cannot guarantee he would see events in the same light. I cannot guarantee his reaction or what...penalty he might deem just."

Thomas turned to face her. "For that reason, I will not insist you accompany me. In fact, I'll ask that you not. I go alone to the king's court. What I offer you is this. I give you six months to follow me there. Until you arrive or until the sixth months expire, I will tell the king I'm awaiting one last piece of information before I can answer the question of Lord Groswick's fate. Should you come, I will go to the king privately, explain what I feel happened, and beg his mercy when you come before him. I will also tell him that it's the deepest wish of my heart—the only thing I want in this life—that we be allowed to marry."

"And..." She had to stop and clear the lump from her throat. "Should I not follow within six months?"

He watched her closely, the gaze of his blue eyes a sword that drove into her heart. "I will tell the king I've received word that Lord Groswick died in an accident at the keep. No word was sent as he lingered for some time, and recovery was uncertain. The king will likely appoint someone to take charge of the keep and its demesne. I will request that he give you some jointure so that your future is secured. As a widow, you will then have the luxury to make what arrangements please you."

She sucked in a breath. "I would not see you again, though."

"I cannot answer that with any certainty."

She considered it for a moment before the realization came to her. "You would lie for me to the king?"

He let out a harsh breath and nodded. "A small evil to prevent the greater one of your being unjustly condemned. My conscience can abide it."

"And I can prevent its necessity."

"Consider well the possible price, my lady," he warned.

"I shall," she promised. "Most surely I shall consider well the price involved either way." Her eyes burned with tears she refused to release.

* * * * *

Thomas left two days later, taking Bertram with him. Ralf had not yet recovered enough to withstand the rigors of travel. He would either make his own way to court later, when he recovered, or accompany Lady Juliana, should she decide to make the journey.

The night before his departure, they undressed each other and lay together, kissing and stroking each other for a long time. His mouth worked hers until she opened for him, and then his tongue plundered every nook and corner.

When he drew back and just watched her for a moment, his head propped on his bent elbow, the candlelight reflected in the gold of his hair and burnished his skin. She'd never seen a man so beautiful before. That he was also strong, honorable, courageous and kind could be nothing less than a miracle. A miracle she didn't deserve.

"Your expression is sad, my love," he said. "Do not think on what is to come. For tonight think only of what we have now."

For his sake she would try. "Kiss me again, then," she begged. "You are most accomplished at distracting me in that way."

"I'm at my lady's command." He leaned down and kissed her again. After ravaging her mouth, he went for her breasts. His tongue swirled around her nipples, sending waves of pleasure singing through her blood. He poked at them, sucked gently, then harder and even nipped them hard enough to sting. It was a thrilling pain that made her quim weep for him.

He rubbed her thighs, brushing up and down the insides, moving higher with each pass until he just slid into her cleft. When she thought she'd go mad, he finally moved higher to dip into the soft, damp folds of her quim. He stroked softly, making her squeal with the pleasure.

"I'll remember this night for a long time," he told her, "and so I'll not move quickly."

He kept that promise. With lazy, tantalizing strokes and nips and soft rubbing, he slowly built the pressure, taking her into a frenzy of heat and desire that mounted so high she couldn't contain it. Whenever she came close to bursting, however, he would stop and wait until she cooled off just enough to prevent her climaxing. Then he would begin again.

Three times he brought her to the edge of exploding and backed off. Juliana thought she would go mad with it, but the fourth time, the pressure grew to a point beyond anything she'd yet experienced. Like a soap bubble expanding, its containment thinned and grew ever more fragile even as the size of it swelled.

When he gave her a pearl a few hard tweaks, it finally exploded. She let out a long, shrill scream as the spasms of release took her to a pleasure beyond anything she'd ever guessed possible before, a perfection of pleasure just this side of heaven. Thomas held her while she bucked and jumped as repeated bursts of rapture broke through her.

It left her breathless and panting, and, when it finally wore itself out, suffused with peace and calm.

"That was truly astonishing," she told him when she could speak again. "You've shown me things I never guessed could be. I cannot begin to thank you for that."

"You needn't. It has been my pleasure as well. You're an apt pupil, and perhaps this makes amends for some of what you suffered at Groswick's hands."

"If 'twas necessary for me to suffer him to know this from you, then 'twas more than worth it." Juliana pulled his face down to kiss him, then she rolled him over so she could have clear access to his body. "Now, let me make more memories for you."

She brushed her fingers through his blond hair, combing out the soft strands, and committing the feel of it to her own stock of memories she'd treasure. She kissed his mouth, his cheeks, the soft skin beneath his ear, down his throat and across his chest. The warmth of his skin, the hardness of muscle rippling beneath it, the way he gasped and jerked in pleasure when she touched his nipples, all those went into the repository as well.

She grazed a palm over his long, strong thighs, rasping on the hair-roughened flesh there. He jumped and sucked in a sharp breath when she touched his balls, cupping them in her hand. His cock jerked at her touch, jumping with eagerness for her pumping. But she, too, tried to keep it slow, to build it deliberately but not too quickly for him.

The sight of his rampant cock filling her hands, the smell of his arousal, the satiny feel of the skin stocked her memory deposit as well. She vowed to remember every square inch of him, every small moan he made, the feel of him throbbing in her clasp.

As the rhythm of her stroking picked up, she found a nipple with her other hand. A swirling touch, a rub, a pinch had him moaning, his face screwed into a frown of concentrated pleasure.

"Ah, please —," he begged. "Don't stop. Please, don't stop."

She didn't. She stroked him faster and faster, matching the bucking rhythm of his body, until he froze, paralyzed in a moment of extreme tension and pleasure, then he jerked several times, hard, and the thick, sticky liquid of his seed spurted from his cock.

His breath came in a series of hard pants, but he drew her up and against his chest, to hold her tight in his arms as he breathed his thanks and love.

"I do love you, you know," he said. "Never have I felt such joy and comfort in a woman's arms, in her very presence. You'll be in my heart all the days of my life."

"As you'll be in mine," she promised.

They fell asleep entwined in each other's arms.

Dawn came too early and with it, he set out with Bertram for the capital and the king.

Though the weather turned reasonably nice for the next week or so, Juliana felt as though Thomas had taken all the sunshine with him when he left. Certainly he took the greater part of her heart. Having him depart so soon after her mother's funeral made her feel particularly bereft and lonely. Though the people of the household were sympathetic and kind, no one could fill the hole in her life left by the absence of her mother and the man she loved. With harvest done and winter setting in, there was less work to fill her time also.

She'd made her decision even before he'd left, but the quiet period offered her space to think about his offer. For a man who hated lies and deceit as much as he did, the fact that he was willing to lie to save her felt like both a sword to the heart and a gift more precious than any she'd ever received.

She couldn't do that to him.

There was more to do than she'd realized, as she began to prepare to leave for a while. It gave her pause. William Randolph could run the keep for a time in her absence, but what if the king did not spare her? What would the people here do? The king would appoint a new lord, but what if he were someone as harsh and cruel as Groswick? What would they do?

Did she have the right to take that chance with the lives and happiness of so many people here? It was an issue she had to weigh more seriously than she would have expected. Perhaps Thomas had seen the possible conflict, and wanted her to have the freedom to make what she considered the best decision. Yet, there was only one choice she could make. Her heart knew it.

Though terrified by visions of what might await her at the end of the journey, Juliana nonetheless desperately wanted to get underway. Every day of delay kept her away from Thomas. Unfortunately, even after she had all in order in the keep, she still had to wait for Ralf to recover enough to travel. The squire had proclaimed himself ready three days after Sir Thomas's departure, but Juliana had watched the young man and seen how quickly he tired from relatively easy tasks like eating dinner.

It took more than two weeks before Ralf could handle the rigors of an hour of sword-training, the mark she'd mentally set for considering him ready to travel. But by then the weather had turned again, with huge gray clouds dropping another blanket of snow on the ground, and cold winds whipping it into perilous drifts.

Continued cold weather meant the snow and ice lingered for another week before melting enough that she could finally plan to set out. Almost half the household approached her during the interval and begged her not to leave, especially not with the Christmas holiday approaching. Juliana heard each one out. After the first couple of times, she stopped trying to explain why she needed to go. They all understood her reasons; they simply wanted her to know how much they would miss her and how much they feared for her.

The longer she had to wait, the more her fear of the journey itself and what awaited her at the end grew. It didn't stop her from leaving as soon as the weather cleared enough to make it possible.

The day she set out, accompanied by Ralf and four men-at-arms from the keeps' guards, the sun shone brightly, but it was cold enough to make her shiver, even within her fur-lined cloak.

It took almost a week to make the journey, and they were seven of the most physically miserable days of her life. After the first day, the sun remained in hiding behind banks of dark clouds, and for two days, a chill rain mixed with ice fell. Most nights they were able to find a town with a tavern where they could spend the night and get warm for a while, but one day the icy rain slowed them so much they didn't make it to a town before dark and had to hastily pitch tents that leaked and barely kept out enough moisture to let them build a smoky fire.

While they traveled, her hands and feet felt frozen most of the time. Wind and rain chafed her face. Her clothes grew damp and uncomfortable. Ralf and the other men did all in their power to ease and protect her, which forced her to maintain a more cheerful attitude than she felt.

The dreary weather put her in an introspective, difficult mood. She couldn't help but consider all the grimmest scenarios about what might happen once she went before the king. Dying she could accept, but she dreaded the thought of torture. And how would Thomas handle her death if the king demanded it?

Despite her fears, the sheer agony of the trip made her grateful when they finally arrived in the city. As he'd done for the entire journey, Ralf led them unerringly as they wound through a maze of narrow, crowded streets, remarkably full of people and noise. Exotic aromas assailed her, some—but not all—of them wafting from the stalls of vendors they pased. People darted out in front of their party, with no apparent care for their likelihood of being knocked over by a horse or cart.

It took an amazingly long time to get to the king's palace. She'd had no idea a city could be so large and so noisy, with so many people crammed together in one place. It couldn't be healthy, surely.

At last, though, they approached an impressive gate. It stood open, and lines of people came and went through it. The palace loomed before them once they passed the entrance, an immense, ornate building with majestic towers and grand banners flanking steps up to the main door. Their party stopped just in front of it, dismounted, and began to ascend the stairs.

A pair of armed guards stopped them and asked their names and business. The mention of Sir Thomas's name bought them entrance and the services of a footman to escort them to a parlor where they might wait while he was summoned.

They didn't wait long. Shortly after a servant arrived with warmed wine and fragrant scones, Sir Thomas himself entered.

The reunion was joyous. Once the squire had greeted his knight, Ralf took the men-at-arms away to show them to their quarters, leaving her alone with Thomas. He pulled her into his arms and kissed her until she felt faint with the delight of it. For her part, Juliana clung to him, content to run her hands up and down his strong back and rest her head on his chest.

Inevitably, though, they had to pull apart and become practical people again. Thomas showed her to chambers he'd reserved for her, and introduced her to Ellyn, the young woman he'd engaged to be her maid.

Shortly thereafter Thomas left her to attend to business. One of those tasks was to secure a private audience with the king as soon as possible. He promised to join her for dinner that evening.

Ellyn helped her settle into her quarters and gave her a tour of the important parts of the palace during the rest of the afternoon. Thomas returned later, and they had a quiet meal together with Ralf and her men-at-arms. She tried to suppress her disappointment when Thomas left after they were done, though she knew it would be inappropriate for him to stay with her here.

The next day, at Thomas's orders, Ellyn took her to a group of seamstresses to get her a pair of new gowns. He wanted her to look every inch a lady when she appeared before the king.

He returned at midday with the news that he'd had a private talk with the king. Juliana's pulse picked up, and the breath caught in her throat as she waited.

Thomas shook his head. "I don't know. I told the king what happened, how I felt about it, and how I felt about you. I told him you wanted to come before him and submit yourself to his judgment. He agreed to hear you. I begged him to be merciful, but he said nothing to me in response and his expression gave me no clue." He stopped and sighed heavily. "I don't know. I can give you no assurances."

The way he paced and the frown on his face showed he needed the reassurance as much as she did. She went to him. Standing behind him, she circled his chest with her arms and rested her head against his back. "God's will shall prevail. And all will be well as a result. I believe he'll grant us mercy."

"I wish I could have your confidence."

"In truth, it's no more than a strong hope. Hope is one of the cardinal virtues. Along with faith and love."

He shrugged in her arms. "I have little of faith, but an excess of love. In between, perhaps I can find some hope, but I fear to trust it too much."

A knock at the door heralded the return of Ellyn, so they stepped apart without either of them affording the other much comfort. Before he left her to dress for her audience with the king, he went over what she needed to know of court etiquette and tried to give her some idea what to expect.

He departed, and Juliana tried not to shake too hard as Ellyn helped her into the most elegant gown she'd ever worn. Deep green velvet had a subtle floral design embroidered with gold thread along its edges. The color made her look a bit pale, but then again, perhaps she was just paler than usual.

As the time drew near, Ellyn escorted her to the doors of the king's audience chamber. A footman answered their knock and nodded when Juliana identified herself.

"Enter, Lady Groswick," he said. "His Majesty awaits you."

Walking the long center aisle of the hall, to the throne at the far end, might have been the hardest thing she ever did. Conversations stopped as she drew near to the throne. She was aware of the presence of other people in the room, quite a number of them, but her attention fixed on the man seated on the throne. He was somewhat beyond middle years, but still vigorous for all that, and his eyes held sharp intelligence.

When she stood in front of the throne, she stopped and dropped into the deepest curtsy she could manage.

"Your Majesty."

"Rise, Lady Groswick," the king said. "Our knight, Sir Thomas Carlwick, advised us of your coming, and that you brought with you the answer to a riddle we've puzzled over for some time."

"Aye, Your Majesty. With your permission, I should like to tell you what happened to my husband, Lord Groswick."

Juliana looked up at the king. His gaze was stern with no encouragement nor any sign of mercy. She nearly lost her nerve and ran from the room. She drew several deep breaths while praying for calm.

"Tell your story, my lady," the king ordered, his voice so expressionless she could derive no guess as to his feelings.

Juliana told him the truth about Groswick's death, the same story she'd told Thomas. She made no effort to excuse her own actions, but she did emphasize that at the time, she very much feared Groswick would kill her. She looked around the court once or twice. Thomas stood off to one side, watching her. His painful dread was almost more than she could bear.

As she turned back to the king, her gaze was met and briefly held by a man standing near the dais. Not a young man, but not old either; he had the stern countenance and confident bearing of a warrior. He wore black from head to foot, and it suited him. Not exactly handsome, he was nonetheless striking and attractive. He was also decidedly intrigued by her, if she judged his expression correctly.

But that could only distract her for a moment. She turned back to face the king and finish her confession. As she ended her story, she added, "Your Majesty, it was not my intention to harm my husband, but harm him I did anyway. I throw myself on your justice and mercy."

Juliana blinked away the tears that threatened to fall and struggled to keep her entire body from trembling. Her knees felt weak and rubbery, a tendency that got worse as the king sat, staring at her, and said nothing. An unsettling silence descended on the hall as all awaited the king's judgment.

Finally the king's mouth squeezed together in a frown. He coughed lightly before he spoke. "We do not like this. 'Tis a wife's duty to submit to her husband, and it does not provide an admirable example for our people when a baron's wife injures him in an effort to resist his will, much less kills him."

Juliana's stomach clenched tight and her throat closed down. It felt as though all her insides folded in on themselves. Her rubbery legs started to buckle. She caught herself, though, and stiffened her spine, her legs, and her dignity. She opened her mouth to protest, then stopped. It wasn't wise to interrupt the king.

Yet that didn't stop the man whose gaze she'd met earlier from standing up at that moment, facing the king, and saying, "Your Majesty, before you give your decision, might I say something?"

The king's expression changed to one of resigned amusement tinged with irritation before he swung to face the speaker. "Of course, Edward." More than a hint of sarcasm tinged the words. "You'd likely say it anyway."

Edward. The black clothes. Of course.

"Thank you, Your Majesty. If I might…" The Black Prince approached her and looked carefully at her for a minute. His gaze focused on the scars. He stood beside her and lifted her arm, placing it on his, then walked forward with her to the foot of the dais and up the first step. They stopped no more than two feet from the throne.

"Your Majesty, please look at the lady's face. I'll wager half your kingdom the scars were put there by Lord Groswick. Is it not so, my lady?"

Still in some shock, she looked at the Prince. "Aye, Your Highness. 'Tis so. But how...?"

"Could I know?" The Prince laughed harshly and with no humor. "I knew your husband, my lady. In truth, I was quite startled to hear a rumor that he'd joined me on the Continent, because he and I both knew that were I down to my last man, I should not accept any offer of service from him."

The king's eyebrows rose. "You despised him that much?"

"He was entirely despicable, Your Majesty. When I heard he'd married, I pitied the lady. Now that I've met her and seen what a sweet and lovely person she is, I'm even more disturbed to consider what she must have suffered at his hands."

"Indeed." The word still held a load of irony. "Your sense of justice and mercy does you credit, Edward. Your patience, however, is even yet in need of practice. Now hear us out, if you please."

The Prince bowed, but remained in place next to Juliana. She welcomed his support. Her knees still didn't feel any too stable.

"As we were saying." The king arched an ironic eyebrow at his son. "'Tis not a good thing for a wife to resist her husband and worse to kill him in the attempt. Yet in this case, it appears Lady Juliana truly had reason to fear for her own life and was defending herself."

The king tapped his chin with a grandly beringed finger. "We cannot let this go completely unanswered, or we shall have ladies the kingdom over feeling they can say nay to their husband, should it please them, and bashing them over the head when their husbands object. 'Twill not do. Yet we cannot condemn the lady too harshly for defending herself."

A few more taps on his chin followed as he considered what to do. Finally, the king's face cleared and he nodded to himself. He looked up and glanced around the court.

"Sir Thomas," he called, finding the person he sought. "Come forward."

Thomas joined them on the steps of the dais, standing on her right side, opposite the Prince on her left. Nonetheless, the king's next words were addressed to her.

"Lady Juliana, as a sign of your penitence for having had a part in your husband's death, it is our order that you complete a pilgrimage to the shrine at Canterbury sometime within the coming year. Since this is a penitential pilgrimage, you will go on foot." The king nodded to himself. "We also feel it necessary that we immediately find another husband for you, one who will be able to take you in hand and teach you a wife's place and duty."

The king looked at Thomas. "Sir Thomas, you've done us good service, but we dare ask one last boon of you. If you're willing, we would have you take this lady for your wife. We realize there is a danger in wedding one who has already contributed to the death of a previous husband, but knowing your prowess in battle, we believe you are adequate to the demand."

His Majesty looked over Juliana and his mouth crooked into a small smile. "Though perhaps, given the lady's beauty, the risks of bedding her may well be outweighed by the pleasure in it." He shrugged and turned again to Thomas. "Will you do this for us?"

Thomas reached out and took Juliana's arm, tucking it into the crook of his. "Aye, Your Majesty. I'll wed the lady."

The king's face broke into a wide smile. "Excellent. We have every confidence in your ability to prevent future incidents of the kind she had with Lord Groswick. We would like you to marry this time tomorrow, right here. We'll be your chief witness."

"I'm very sensible of the honor you do us, Your Majesty," Thomas said.

"Aye, just so." He raised one ironic eyebrow for a moment, then grew serious again. "We make it your duty to ensure she makes the pilgrimage we've designated. We trust you'll also discipline her as necessary and care for her as she deserves."

"I give my word on it, Your Majesty."

"Excellent. Sir Thomas, we've been pleased with your service, and grateful for it. You've fulfilled the mission we set for you admirably, and have just now done us an additional boon. Your faithfulness has earned reward." The king tapped his chin again. "We have now a keep with no lord at Groswick. You've seen this keep, Sir Thomas. What think you of it?"

"For the last year or more, the keep has been well managed, Your Majesty, though prior to that, I understand, there were difficulties. The keep I sheltered in for several weeks was a prosperous and well-favored place."

"Excellent. You will not, then, deem it too great a burden should we name you Baron Groswick and give the care of this keep into your hands?"

Thomas drew a sharp breath. "I should be exceedingly honored and grateful, Your Majesty."

"Aye, well, you understand the responsibilities and obligations that accompany the appointment."

"I do, Your Majesty."

"Very well. Go then, both of you. Prepare for your wedding tomorrow. Lady Juliana... We've given you to a husband both strong and worthy. See that you honor him as is his due."

Juliana smiled at Thomas before she answered. "You may depend on it, Your Majesty."

"Very well, then. We're sure you have much to settle between you."

Before she stepped down, Juliana turned to the Prince, who had remained beside her throughout the king's exchange with Thomas. "Your Highness, I'm exceedingly grateful for your assistance."

"It was our pleasure," the Prince assured her. "Go now and be happy with Sir Thomas. You'll find in him all that was lacking in Groswick."

The Prince went back to his seat near the side of the dais. Still arm in arm, Juliana and Thomas walked out of the room. In a daze of disbelief and astonishment, they made it back to her quarters, dismissed Ellyn, and barred the door behind them before Juliana flung herself into his arms and pressed herself against his chest.

"Is it true?" she asked him, "Can it possibly be true? I am allowed to live? And we're ordered to wed on the morrow. I can scarce credit I'm not dreaming it. And you've been made Lord Groswick. The people will rejoice."

"Perhaps as much because they'll continue to have you for their lady as for acquiring me as lord."

"Nay, not so. They do admire you. The guards you've trained have great praise for you. And all the household respects you as well."

"Except for Peter Randolph," Thomas pointed out.

"Aye, well. Except for Peter. But if you return as my savior rather than my potential doom, I think in time even he will be reconciled."

"He'll be reconciled if he wishes to remain at the keep," Thomas said. And then he leaned down to kiss her, and they didn't speak again for a while.

The kiss sent its usual waves of fire pouring down her back and into her gut. She couldn't get close enough to him and lifted his court tunic and shirt to get her hands on his chest. He tugged at tapes and laces. A few hectic, occasionally awkward and tangled moments ensued as they shed their clothes.

Relief and the lifting of long built-up tension made Juliana light-headed, almost giggly. Thomas didn't seem to mind, though, that getting him wrapped up in his own shirt made her dissolve into laughter. He smiled on her mirth and mussed up her hair, tugging it free of the pins that held it up, in revenge for her pulling on his as she finally got the shirt over his head.

He buried his fingers in the released tresses and drew her to him for another long, deep kiss. She drank in the sweetness of that joining, knowing she'd never tire of it and never get enough of it. His jutting cock pressed into her belly. Hands roved over her back, running up and down her spine, then moving around her sides to stroke her breasts. She met his eyes and got lost in the fiery blue depths of them. This man was her fate, her destiny, the one she'd love, honor, and cherish forever.

They tipped over onto the bed in another awkward tangle of limbs. It set her laughing again. Between giggles, she tried to apologize. "I feel like a silly child, laughing over the most ridiculous things. I cannot seem to help it. The relief is so great."

His smile was tender and indulgent as he traced the outline of her lips with a finger. "I like to hear you laugh. I'm sure you've done little enough of it in your life."

Then he ran a hand down over her breast, brushing the nipple, and the jolting pleasure of it chased away the laughter, replacing it with a sharp gasp. He teased the peak with his fingers, then with his tongue, until it stood up hard and she was squirming beneath him. Fire lit the blood in her veins to a boil.

He licked down her stomach, stopping to dip into her belly button, and continued downward to her cleft. Juliana held her breath. His clever mouth explored the petals of her quim before his tongue speared through them and dove deep into her. She gasped and wound her fingers tightly in his hair, holding him to her. With sharp little flicks, he teased her pearl until she writhed with the extremity of sensation.

When he drew back and moved so he could kiss her mouth again, she tasted her own juices on his lips.

Wanting, needing to return the pleasure, she grasped his cock and began to caress it with her fingers. When he moaned softly, it thrilled her to know she could give him pleasure equal to what he brought her. Touching his flesh in this intimate way sent shivers rushing up and down her. The hardness of his need roused an equal response in her. Her quim swelled and tightened, demanding the fulfillment of his invasion. She wanted him, but, even more, she wanted to give him every pleasure possible in return.

Indulging a sudden impulse, she leaned over and pressed her lips to his cock. He gasped sharply. "Does it please you?" she asked.

He had to take a deep breath before he could answer. "More than I can say."

With the tip of her tongue, she licked up along its length to the soft sleek bulb at the top. A drop of liquid oozed from the tiny hole. He groaned when she tasted it. She cupped his balls in her palm, kneading them carefully as she brushed across the sensitive ridges and folds of his cock.

After a moment, he stilled her. "No more, Juliana. No more, lest I explode right now. Turn over."

Instead, she paused and levered herself up on her elbow, looking him in the face. "We're to be married tomorrow, my love. Can we not share fully this evening?"

"But what if I disappoint you? Will you refuse to accept me tomorrow?" Sparkly lights danced in his blue eyes as he teased her.

"I don't believe the king would allow it," she mused. "But it will not be. You couldn't disappoint me. The man you are is all I will ever want."

"As you are the lady I've waited and searched for so long."

He reached down to her quim and dipped his finger into the sensitive folds of flesh there. He found her bud and teased it until she squealed. His stroking of her pearl brought her to a shivering tension that demanded his intrusion for completion.

"Please, Thomas," she begged. "Come into me."

His cock bobbed in her hand, eager to spear her. Thomas gathered some of the moisture seeping from her on his fingers and spread it on the end. Then he moved to position himself over her. The tip of his cock sought for the entrance, and finding it, began to nudge itself in.

It was uncomfortable for a moment or two as she adjusted to his size, which stretched her. He waited patiently for her to signal her readiness to continue. When she relaxed and smiled at him, he pushed deeper and deeper until he was buried in the depths of her body. Her womb swelled around him and spasms jolted through it that held him tight as her arms wound around him to keep him close to her.

He watched her steadily. The love and joy in his expression was an added pleasure in the steadily growing tempest of desire. The fire that burned in him spread to her and blazed through her, a shared benediction of the spirit that joined them.

He withdrew partway, then slid back in. It drew another spasm of pleasure, this time from deep within her womb. When he saw that it pleased her, he drew back and pushed in again, harder this time.

His face scrunched up with joyful strain as he thrust into her again and again.

Tension built inside her as though she ascended a steep hill. Each pleasurable spasm took her higher and higher, increasing the anticipation of getting to the top. Her back arched; she surged upward to meet his thrusts and bounced in a small, needy spasm when his cock hit its home inside. Her fingers dug into his back as the tension grew so huge, she could scarce bear it.

As she neared the peak, her breath couldn't come fast enough. The need demanded he go faster and faster.

Just as she was about to reach the top, he withdrew and stopped partway out for a long breathless, moment. They shared a look steeped in shared love, endless promise, and desperate need for each other. Then he thrust into her again, deep, deeper, deepest. It sent her to the top of the hill and over.

Huge spasms rolled over her, making her jolt and buck against him. He grunted deep in his throat with the explosive relief of his tension. They held onto each other while each rocked with the joy of their mutual climax. She didn't so much roll down off the top of the hill as float down from it.

The peace that filled her as the spasms of release began to abate was like nothing she'd ever experienced. It held fulfillment, and love, and a saturating joy.

Thomas collapsed on top of her. His dear weight pressed against her chest and belly, while his head fit into her shoulder, his face alongside hers, cheek to cheek. It interfered with her breathing, but she didn't care. If she were to die this way, she would die happy, but she knew he wouldn't allow that to happen. They held onto each other and their complete, perfect melding of two individuals into one. It wouldn't last, but the memories and renewals of it would.

Finally, he pushed himself off and rolled over to lay beside her. He took her hand. "Juliana, as God is my witness, you are my lady, my wife. You're mine from this moment on. I promise to love, protect, cherish and honor you for the rest of our lives."

She looked into his blue eyes as she brought her other hand over to cover their joined ones. "Thomas, as God is my witness, you are my love and my husband from this moment on. I promise to love, honor, and cherish you as well for the rest of our lives."

Tomorrow they'd make those vows in front of witnesses, where they would be legally binding. But these were the vows that would bind their hearts and souls for the rest of their lives.

"And now that we've slaked the most immediate desperate need, we have yet all night for more," he said. "I plan to take you more slowly next time. I want to touch every square inch of you and kiss it as well. I want to show you a thousand more delights. I hope you have no plans to sleep tonight, my love."

Juliana touched his cheek, and ran her hand down his chest to his already swelling cock. Love for him swelled so full in her breast, she wondered she didn't burst with it. "None whatsoever, my husband."

Enjoy this excerpt from:
EQUINOX
WALPURGIS NIGHT

© Copyright Katherine Kingston 2003

"Who will it be?" Jerrod added. "Tonight you must choose one of us."

It was so, and that was just the reason she'd tried to remain out of sight. She would have hidden in Marla's home had she not suspected they would search the place for her. In fact, they were so intent on having her, they'd have searched every building in town and the surrounding hills. She'd gambled that by staying near the center of activity, but concealed in shadows, she might remain hidden. One small lapse of attention had overset the plan.

"Choose, witch," they taunted her. "Or perhaps you prefer to be truly branded witch and face the fire."

She glanced at the bonfire and tried to keep the terror from showing too clearly on her face. Surely there was some other way. Fianna let her gaze roam around the square, watching the gathered crowds. Evidently they'd decided the Norsemen posed no threat. Most had resumed their revelry, laughing, dancing, and flirting.

She spotted the Norsemen not far away. Someone had passed them a wineskin, and one of the three was drinking from it. A wild idea formed in her head.

"Choose me and I'll make you roar and scream with delight," Jerrod promised, drawing her attention back to her tormentors.

"I have the equipment of a bull and I'll fill you properly," Artur boasted.

Keovan couldn't match his companion's physical assets and attempted a different form of persuasion. "I've a gold chain brought from the east that can be yours, do you go with me this night," he offered.

Fianna glanced at each one and then at the others in the square. The leader of the Norsemen glanced her way and met her eyes briefly, but he clearly decided their doings were none of his concern.

"I've made my choice," Fianna announced to the group. All three stared at her. She glanced at each in turn, then shifted her gaze away from them.

"Him," she said, pointing to the leader of the Norsemen.

While Artur, Jerrod, and Keovan still stared blankly at her, she pushed past them and walked toward the visitors.

The Norsemen's eyebrows all rose in surprise as she approached them. Fianna ignored all but the man in the middle, keeping her gaze locked with his as she neared. "You are my choice," she said to him, making the words loud enough to be heard by the small group of men following her as well as those in front.

"You're Henrik," she said to him. "Nay?"

"Aye, lady," he acknowledged. "And you are?"

"Fianna."

"Ah. And for what purpose do you choose me?"

This close to him, she had to look up to see his face. His expression remained so shuttered she read nothing in it, nor did his tone reveal any emotion save mild curiosity.

"To be my…companion for the night." She wasn't sure what word to use that he would understand. She wasn't sure she wanted to use any word at all. As she faced this stern, intimidatingly large, strong man, Fianna asked herself whether this had been a good idea. It got her out of the reach of Jerrod and his fellows, but it might leave her in an even more dangerous situation.

"Your companion?" Henrik scanned the square, taking in the revelers, his gaze coming to rest on one couple all but undressing each other in the street. The woman's leg was over the man's bent knee, and one of his hands rested high on her thigh while the other pushed aside her bodice so he could reach her breast. The woman, meanwhile, had both hands pressed against his chest under his shirt.

While he stared, Fianna wondered what she'd do if he turned her down. She supposed she would have to choose one of the group that still stood behind her, waiting to see how this would play out.

"Why do you ask this of me?" Suspicion almost overwhelmed the curiosity in his tone.

"You are a man," she answered. "I am a woman. And on this night it is said that all must pay homage to the spirits that control the fertility of the land." She wasn't sure how much he understood of her language.

When he commented, "And you think I'm the best of the choices you have," she decided it wouldn't be wise to underestimate him.

He looked at the group of ardent suitors standing behind her, and his face softened a fraction out of its hard set. "You don't know what you risk with me."

She puzzled at that. "Nay. But I know what I risk with others."

His eyebrows flicked upward. He leaned forward to whisper to her. "You cannot know how I prefer to enjoy a woman."

"Nay, that I do not," she admitted. "What should I know?"

His expression grew darker. "I do not prefer it quick. Or gentle. I like women who will give everything to me, and accept all I want to do to them. Think you, you can do this? Or are you wishing to change your choice?"

"Do your women survive their time with you?"

He laughed suddenly. "Usually. In truth, none have died of the things I do with them, though I've seen a few swoon. Most seem quite pleased and satisfied with our time together. Not all can satisfy me, however."

She looked at him. He thought he was frightening her. And she should be heeding his warning. But along with the fear was something else. Her stomach did odd little flip-flops, while a frisson of excitement settled hard and heavy in her loins. "I will do my best, though I can make no promises until I know more of what you want."

"'Tis just for this night?"

"This one night only," she assured him.

He stared hard into her eyes, as though trying to read her will. "You interest me, Fianna. I will accept your offer."

Fianna let out a long sigh, though she wondered if relief was truly the proper reaction. She just knew that if she had to give herself to one man, this was the one who seemed most appealing. Oddly, his words about his possibly unusual preferences made the prospect of time with him more appealing rather than less.

He said a few words in his own language to his companions. One of those two laughed hard and struck him on the back. The other looked suspicious. A brief argument between that one and Henrik ended with the man pronouncing something she couldn't understand. She could read the tone, however, and he'd clearly said something on the order of, "On your own head be it."

Henrik's companions moved away to leave him alone with her. The man glared at Jerrod, Artur, and Keovan until they, also, got the message and retreated. Then he bent his stare on her again.

Fianna studied his face, trying to decide how worried she should be. His features were strong, from the straight, gold eyebrows to the firm, jutting chin outlined by a neatly clipped golden beard. In the firelight she couldn't tell the color of his eyes, only that they were light. A bit of satisfaction had leeched into his otherwise set expression.

"So, lady," he said, "What do we now?"

"We go some place private."

"Know you such a place nearby?"

She nodded. "My quarters. I share a home with Marla, the midwife, but I have my own room."

"Let us go then." He took a torch from one of the many stands holding them and nodded for her to direct him.

The house was quiet and dark. Marla was probably with Master Cooper at his place. They'd been lovers for years, though Marla refused to marry him, claiming she was content with her living arrangements as they were.

Fianna lit a lamp and carried it back to her private room. Henrik put the torch into a stand, then glanced around the room. She wondered what he thought of her very spare quarters, but she didn't ask and he volunteered no opinion. He paid little attention to it in any case. His gaze returned to her and stayed there. She blushed when he looked slowly down her body. She hoped her shape pleased him. Most men seemed to consider her attractive, but the Norsemen might have different notions of beauty.

Fianna had no idea what to do next, what he might expect of her, so she waited for him to make the first move. Henrik unbuckled his belt and slid the sheath holding his sword off it, laid both aside, and then removed his leather vest and shirt.

She let out a gasp of pure wonder as she stared at the most beautiful masculine chest she'd ever seen. Broad shoulders narrowed gradually down to a slim waist and hard, flat belly. A thin mat of gold hair lay over the strong muscles below his throat, with the dark buds of nipples protruding from it. The lovely flesh almost demanded she touch it, but something in his expression prevented her from reaching out.

"Have you done this before?" he asked.

"Aye. Once or twice."

"No more than that?" He sounded incredulous.

"No more."

"Did you take pleasure from it?"

She drew a deep breath and let it out slowly. She hated to be found wanting, but neither did she wish to lie to him. "Nay, in truth, I found little, though I'm told it should be pleasurable."

"So it should," he agreed. "And you will get pleasure from it with me. But you must first agree that I am your master in this and you will do all I say without hesitation or question." He stopped and drew a breath. "I warned you my needs and desires were different. This I ask of you, that you agree I am your lord for this night and you must obey all orders or face my punishment for the failure." His harsh expression softened. "I know it is not easy for one of your spirit to submit yourself to another's will. But I believe I can show you the way to greater pleasure than you've ever known."

The demand left her breathless and confused, while his promise set off that funny feeling in her stomach.

"Fianna?" he prompted. "Do you agree?"

"If I don't?"

"I'll put my clothes back on and go. But I'll stay out of sight so those men will believe I'm with you still."

She was stunned by that bit of proposed gallantry. But she hadn't been clear about her question and tried to clarify. "Nay. I mean if I agree and then I don't follow orders? How would you punish me?" she asked.

"Ah." A gleam lit his eyes. "What do you suppose I should do?"

The heat rose in her cheeks, so she must be blushing. A vivid image had come into her mind, and she wasn't sure whether it fascinated or terrified her. It depended on how much she trusted him. But—he had asked.

"I know not," she said, hoping she wasn't making a terrible mistake. "What were you thinking?"

He stared hard at her as though he tried to read her mind through her eyes. "Perhaps I'll spank your bottom until it glows pink. Or possibly I'll use my belt, doubled over. Which frightens you more?"

She sucked in a sharp breath, but she wasn't sure whether the twisting feeling in her stomach was dismay or excitement. "The belt," she whispered.

He nodded. "Do you agree, then?"

"But you didn't—"

"And I will not. You know enough to make your decision."

How could she be so thrilled and so terrified at the same time? But when she looked at him, stared into his eyes, she knew he wouldn't hurt her. And she knew she wanted this more than she'd ever wanted anything with a man before. Even so, she had a hard time making herself say it. "Aye," she finally managed to choke out.

For the first time a real smile washed across his face. It transformed his features, turning him into a breathtakingly handsome man. Her heart hammered in her chest.

"Good," he said. "Very good. Take off your dress. Slowly."

About the author:

Katherine Kingston welcomes mail from readers. You can write to her c/o Ellora's Cave Publishing at 1337 Commerce Drive, Suite 13, Stow OH 44224.

Also by Katherine Kingston:

Binding Passion
Crown Jewels
Daring Passion
Equinox
Ruling Passion
Silverquest

Why an electronic book?

We live in the Information Age—an exciting time in the history of human civilization in which technology rules supreme and continues to progress in leaps and bounds every minute of every hour of every day. For a multitude of reasons, more and more avid literary fans are opting to purchase e-books instead of paperbacks. The question to those not yet initiated to the world of electronic reading is simply: *why?*

1. *Price.* An electronic title at Ellora's Cave Publishing runs anywhere from 40-75% less than the cover price of the <u>exact same title</u> in paperback format. Why? Cold mathematics. It is less expensive to publish an e-book than it is to publish a paperback, so the savings are passed along to the consumer.

2. *Space.* Running out of room to house your paperback books? That is one worry you will never have with electronic novels. For a low one-time cost, you can purchase a handheld computer designed specifically for e-reading purposes. Many e-readers are larger than the average handheld, giving you plenty of screen room. Better yet, hundreds of titles can be stored within your new library—a single microchip. (Please note that Ellora's Cave does not endorse any specific brands. You can check our website at www.ellorascave.com for customer

recommendations we make available to new consumers.)

3. *Mobility.* Because your new library now consists of only a microchip, your entire cache of books can be taken with you wherever you go.

4. *Personal preferences are accounted for.* Are the words you are currently reading too small? Too large? Too…**ANNOYING**? Paperback books cannot be modified according to personal preferences, but e-books can.

5. *Innovation.* The way you read a book is not the only advancement the Information Age has gifted the literary community with. There is also the factor of what you can read. Ellora's Cave Publishing will be introducing a new line of interactive titles that are available in e-book format only.

6. *Instant gratification.* Is it the middle of the night and all the bookstores are closed? Are you tired of waiting days—sometimes weeks—for online and offline bookstores to ship the novels you bought? Ellora's Cave Publishing sells instantaneous downloads 24 hours a day, 7 days a week, 365 days a year. Our e-book delivery system is 100% automated, meaning your order is filled as soon as you pay for it.

Those are a few of the top reasons why electronic novels are displacing paperbacks for many an avid reader. As always, Ellora's Cave Publishing welcomes your questions and comments. We invite you to email us at service@ellorascave.com or write to us directly at: 1337 Commerce Drive, Suite 13, Stow OH 44224.